Metal Fish, Falling Snow

Cath Moore is of Irish/Afro-Caribbean heritage. She was born in Guyana, raised in Australia and has lived in Scotland and Belgium. She now lives in Melbourne. Cath is an award-winning screenwriter, a teacher and a filmmaker. *Metal Fish, Falling Snow* is her first novel.

Metal Fish, Falling Snow

Cath Moore

TEXT PUBLISHING MELBOURNE AUSTRALIA

textpublishing.com.au

The Text Publishing Company
Swann House, 22 William Street, Melbourne Victoria 3000, Australia

Published by The Text Publishing Company, 2020

Book design by Jessica Horrocks
Cover images by oxygen/Getty and iStock
Typeset in Stempel Garamond 11.5/17 by Duncan Blachford, Typography
Studio

Printed and bound in Australia by Griffin Press, part of Ovato, an accredited
ISO/NZS 14001:2004 Environmental Management System printer.

ISBN: 9781922330079 (paperback)
ISBN: 9781925923513 (ebook)

A catalogue record for this book is available from the National Library of
Australia.

For Ishika and Felix

1

The running wolf

I could be anywhere. Shadows from flickering tree branches dance across the bed and the floor is littered with a mountain of junk parts. Aha, now I know. Bits and pieces of the world Pat has collected, sure he can make them new again if he just tightens a screw. True enough, machines are only alive if we want them to be. They have a different system inside that can be *manip-ulated.* And there he is, in the middle of the kitchen flipping bacon like a pancake. Fat spits onto his arm but Pat doesn't even flinch.

'Siddown.' Pat's not one for hairs and graces. Not at 6 am in the morning. There are fried eggs too. I break the yolk and watch as it runs the wrong way down my plate.

'From now on, you eat what you're given and ya don't play with your food,' Pat says real quiet.

'But it's moving south.' I knife the bacon rind off and put it under the runny yolk. It stops going any further, so I eat the bacon and leave the yellow puddle, even though it's the best part of the egg.

'You finish that plate. It's a long drive.' Pat scrapes his knife like fingernails on a blackboard. Joelle Parkinson did that once because she thought it would make us squirm but in the end she bent a nail backwards and cried.

I try to finish my eggs I really do, but Pat's in a mood and I can't tell him that his forks are the wrong kind of metal. The thin kind that gives my teeth a headache. I took a fork from home but right now I don't know where it is. We had a complete set of estate cutlery. Bought it from Mr and Mrs Dickson when they both went into a nursing home 'cause they'd forgotten who the other one was. Even though they'd been married for sixty-eight years. Kept ringing the police on each other, screaming that there was a burglar in the house. Mrs Dickson even hit Herbert on the head once with a 500-gram tin of home-brand peaches in syrup. But I'm happy we got their forks because they were proper good. Heavy with a fancy D engraved on the end so it looked like they were supposed to be mine all along.

It's a dragon-breath morning. Fingers so cold they don't feel like a part of my body. I stand on the front porch trying to tap some warmth into my toes and start the motor in my heart. It's a morning so quiet you'd think we'd already been forgotten. Or were never here at all. But a town like this doesn't wake up just to say goodbye. And maybe that's okay because for now it's all mine. The maggies with their morning song, warbling joy into the pale blue sky. Dewy spiderwebs all over the bushes, each one like a perfect equation. Across and down the road little Jackson and his dad are walking to their car.

'But I don't have anything for show and tell!'

'Well you can't take a pot plant. Make something up.'

His dad trips over a garden gnome. 'Shit,' he says with the volume turned down. I can hear the garbo coming too; scratching a mole on the back of his neck that's been bothering him for weeks. Then a car door slams behind me and rattles the porch windows. My maggies fly off to find some worms and the spiders pack up their webs.

'Dylan!'

Even though my name swings both ways, the doctor told everyone I was going to be a boy. Probably thought he saw a willy on the ultra-song that was actually just my little finger in the wrong place at the wrong time. 'That's *deception*,' my dad said when he found out I was me instead of a son, and drove off for a few days. But he came back and said they still had to call me Dylan because it was a good, strong name. Plus it was the name of his friend who was in jail and he'd sent me a baseball cap with *Little Dylan* on it.

'Come on, quick sticks,' says Pat. He looks at the ground, says we'd best get going but his words fall into the hole he's diggin' with his boot.

I wanna slip into those dry cracks and stay put. Lie in the ground with Mama. But I know the earth and this town are only for those who belong. And without someone to love, you can't belong anywhere.

We're leaving this back-paddock town. As you hit the main drag there's a sign that says 'Welcome to Beyen! *Keep driving*.' Mitchell Baker who's always selling homemade cigarettes round the back of the bike shed wrote that last part, with a black marker he stole from the art room. It's true, though. You can miss this town and not miss a thing. It's where I've long been but never belonged. Not like Piper or Lily or the Magann twins. Their families go way back to the beginning of time and even then, people are still calling them coon and Abo like they shouldn't be here either. My time is up before it really began and I can't say I'm too glum about that. I am sad to leave Mum behind though, because now she'll always be part of this town even though no one will ever see her again.

Before I made a mess of it all, Mum and I were gonna sail back to her belonging. Back to where she'd been a happy little girl drinking hot chocolate out of a bowl and skipping to school with a big chunk of stinky cheese in her bag. Mum missed Paris so much it felt like she'd pulled a muscle in her heart and some days she would just curl up on the bed trying to remember what cold felt like. It was never really winter in Beyen—I couldn't imagine snow falling from the sky. Each flake one-of-a-kind, like a frozen fingerprint that only lives between the sky and the earth.

We really were gonna make it happen. Get away from the heat and the flies and the non-belonging that was always making us feel heavy here in Beyen.

I know Mum is in the ground now, but I still need to take her home. Because we are more than our bodies.

Tiffany who runs *Mysticize*, the candle and crystal shop above the Chinese takeaway, told me Mum's spirit was free now, so all I'm thinking about is getting her to the water. I've never seen the sea, felt the waves slap onto my back, saltwater spray across my face. The town pool in Beyen isn't the same. Most of the time it's only half-full and you can always tell when Ash Malone's done a stinky wee in the deep end.

It's a long way from Beyen to the ocean. It's numbers ticking over and over on the dashboard and a whole lot of sleeps trying to dream yourself there. And I have, because it's the only thing that matters if you want to stay real.

The land out here is a sea of dry dust. It covers the ground and stops living things from breathing. Nothing comes out of the earth and the only things that go in are bones and history, death and regret. That's what the old men propping up the front bar say when they're talkin' themselves through another pint of stout.

Water is a miracle. What else can slip through your hands or crush you in two seconds flat? What else is soft and strong enough to carve patterns into stone? It regulates, generates and lubricates body parts we didn't even know we had. Babies are seventy-eight per cent water when they are born. The older we get the less we have. Right now I'm only about fifty-five per cent. That's all teenage girls have. But when I get to the sea, the salty air will fill my lungs up like a petrol pump and maybe my numbers will change. Mum used to say that everyone's soul is connected to water because it's a life force.

Even though Paris is a dirty city far from the ocean. The sea is always a passage home.

Water is where this story begins and ends. A question chasing its tail for the answer. And what lies in the middle? Well I'll save that for the car ride. Pat was right about that. It's a long trip. He locks up the house, flicking pieces of dry paint off the porch. Stares at his hand, a few red specks caught under the nails. And I reckon that's about all he's taking from the place. If I squint hard enough, I can see Barry standing tall in the field at the bottom of Novis Lane. Now you might think I'm silly for naming a tree. Wouldn't be the first time I've been called dumb as a stump, or smart as a stick. Duncan Glover used to call me a teabag: takes a while for things to filter through. But Barry's not a regular tree; he's where I used to go and hide myself. Barry knows I'm going now. He knows what happened too.

Pat catches my eyes on him and brushes something invisible from his pants.

'You remember everything?'

Suddenly I'm afraid. Have I packed all the knowledge?

''Cause we're not comin' back,' he says with a big fat full stop.

'But I don't know all the galaxies or what disease emphysema is.'

Pat rolls his eyes.

I've got it wrong again. People don't always use words to say what they think. Sometimes it can be a long unblinking stare from the other side of Parker Street one Tuesday arvo that burns like a branding iron. 'Go back' is what those eyes mark on your shadow so you're always in the wrong place no matter where you are. Right now I'm using that eye-talk with Pat. He hasn't said anything about the boat so I don't know if he thinks he's coming too. I give him this cowboy glare that says 'Sorry mate it's not on the cards. Not even the four of spades. This is a family trip and you and me are not that.'

I know the boat will be made out of metal. Or wood. I just don't know where it is yet. But I will *feel it in my waters* as Margie says about the rain that mostly always never comes. She's eighty-nine and has lived in Beyen forever. This town is the beginning, middle and end of the whole world for her. Margie's life map is very small but mine is just about to start. A single crack in the dry earth travelling east from the middle of nowhere to the wide, open sea.

Sometimes I find my way into memories that aren't mine. Saturday just gone I walked past a lady picking up pork ribs from Gary the butcher, and suddenly I'm at her kitchen table watching as she plays gin rummy with the girls, cackling like galahs when Theodora says that Ian sleepwalked into the kitchen and peed into the geranium pot by the window but, gee, hasn't it flowered well since then. I'm only there for a few seconds before I get sucked back out, but I know a lot of people in this town and the secret things they do. I didn't ask for that kind of knowing and sometimes I wish I could shut it off, especially when I see things I don't want to. Like Mr Kelly's grandson who lives in Adelaide but comes here for the holidays. I passed him one day sitting on the front porch. Looked into his eyes and watched as he drowned a cat in a bucket of water behind Mr Kelly's back shed. It was all gone in a flash and when I looked back at him sitting on the porch, he held up a kitten for me to see. Cuddled it close to his chest and smiled.

I had a kitty once, called Ashtray. He'd cuddle close to me as well, purr loud as a lawnmower. Did Mr Kelly's grandson know that too? People like him are why you keep your eyes to yourself. When I told Mum about the things I saw, I thought she'd say, 'It's only a hop, skip and a jump from heaven to hell for telling a lie.' But she whispered that life was full of things we could not understand. That it must be hard to suddenly see a glimpse of what makes people tick, for better or worse.

I won't be taking any of those memories with me if I can help it. Got no room for drowned cats or pot-plant pee.

Brown foam bulges out from under the wrecked car-seat cover and I think the whole world is second-hand. What does new smell and look like? How do you feel if you're pretty? The engine chokes on its own smoke and splutters into action. We pull out and follow the sun as it rises. No one but us, like we called ahead and booked out the whole damn road. If we were bandits on the run, we'd have special names like Fury and the Tadpole. Or Buster and the Choc Drop. But in this bomb-of-a-ute, held together with rust and rubber bands, it's just me and Pat and the only thing chasing us is a tornado of dust. It spurts out from the tyres and hits the back window like a hazy brown blanket.

You'd think it just being the two of us we'd have a cracker of a conversation going but Pat's sold all his words for a big slice of silence. Clenches the wheel so hard it looks like his knuckles are gonna pop through the skin. And when someone has angry hands you don't talk. But I know we're thinking the same thing— that it's my fault she's not here. True enough, I've never been very good at keeping people around and now I'm basically an orphan. Although Pat's grumpy like Daddy Warbucks (without the bucks) it's really not at all like *Annie*.

Pat's not my dad. He's Mum's boyfriend. *Was*. Now everything is past and I'm not sure what he is to me. Or vice versa.

Dad's the one who made me black. A darkness so deep down you cannot take it out or scrape it off.

Besides I'm fourteen and by now it's probably seeped into my bone marrow. Even though Mum had the safe kind of skin, I only got it on my palms and the soles of my feet. Not much good there. Maybe none of that matters anymore because this is the end of the beginning.

We're coming up to the Red River Hotel. Might as well have been Pat's second home. I bet he's scared that the magic will happen without him. But just because you believe in something, doesn't make it true. Mum said he was stupid to fill a metal box with a gas bill or a week's worth of shopping. Pat goes there a lot because he can't sleep and the lights are so bright that night is always day. They all know his name, the tap beer he likes and the pokie where he has to sit. One time he got into a fight because Les was at his machine, so Pat tipped Les's cup on the floor and everyone scrambled to pick up the coins like they were piñata lollies.

But the Red River's also where Mum used to work. She was only supposed to stay for a year, making her way around Australia one pub at a time. Mum was like some kind of exotic bird with her French accent. They used to joke about lining the floor of the bar with mattresses on account of all the fellas falling head over heels. Including my dad. And, even though there are black people in Paris, maybe he was kind of exotic to Mum too. At first they got on lovely because Dad wanted to make a go of it for real. But there was a complicated knot in Dad's head, and when it got too twisted, things got bad. Snap, bang, heart's in your mouth pounding like a racehorse. A hand whips across Mum's face and she holds her cheek, red with slap burn. Dad slams the door so hard the whole house shakes.

Dad gave me my skin. It's not really his fault though 'cause he got the blackness from *his* dad. That's called a legacy, which is usually a good thing like having a five-octave singing voice or being double-jointed. I can only click my knuckles when it gets real cold. Mum kept saying my skin was special, that it brought people and places together. 'Who and where?' I used to ask, but she'd just look out the window at something that wasn't there. Mum didn't want to scare me but I already knew.

My grandad William Freeman is a bottom-of-the-well kind of black. Darkly deep and deeply dark, a no-way-out kind of black that cracks the pavement wide open and swallows you whole. That kind of legacy's no good. Neither is my surname. I don't know why I got stuck with Freeman because I don't feel free at all, having this blackness weigh me down. Even though my skin is one shade lighter than my dad's and two shades lighter than William Freeman's, it's still dark enough to bring me trouble. Back gate banging in the wind. Black like a wolf running through the night panting with hunger. It might tear down the door with its sharp nails and turn into a ball of smoke, which I'd accidentally breathe in. Have that wolf hibernate in my chest and make me do bad things. When I told Mum about the smoky wolf she took me to a lady doctor to have a chat about it all, but she just sat there and made me play with emotion-face cards. Like I was a baby or something. The blackness always made me feel wrong. Sometimes we'd go for a walk and people would look at me and then glance at Mum. Like we didn't fit together. Once, a fat boy with a yellow front tooth rode past on a bike and called me Sambo. It sounded like a pretty word but Mum chased after him. Couldn't hear what she said but that boy turned around and stared me down for the longest time. He saw the wolf and the wolf saw him.

Another time on a school trip to the Blue Mountains these two men said I should go back to where I came from. I said we weren't going home 'til Tuesday but that was the wrong answer because they laughed. They said I was from Africa, but that's not true. I'm from Beyen. And how could I get to Africa anyway? I don't have a passport or anyone to stay with. I know they think brown skin is always 'somewhere else' on a map. But I can't say mine comes from Guyana because when I do people always crinkle their eyes and say 'Ghana?' like they just haven't heard me right. Then I have to say 'No, that's in Africa, Guyana is in South America.' And I'm tired of talking about that map and all the different consonants. *Continents*. I didn't think those men would care anyway so I just kept my mouth shut and looked at the ground for a very long time.

At the YMCA hostel that night there was unlimited soft drink top-ups. Normally I would've been up for an alphabet burping competition because I can usually get to J. But on that particular night if you'd opened me up, you would've seen that big old wolf howling at the moon. Alone and lonely (at the same time). Brown is a loud colour to wear on your face. I get onto a crowded bus and everyone looks up at me like they've heard my skin arrive. 'What are you doing here?' their blank stares say. 'Turn that pigment down!'

If you didn't already know, skin has a lifetime colour guarantee. Once I got a whole box of scouring pads from under the kitchen sink and tried to scrape the brown off my arms. I wanted my skin to grow back white so I could be beautiful like Mum. So when we sailed back to France no one would look at us funny and I could blend in like white people do. But when the gauze pads came off it was just the same brown again, full of scabs. So as much as possible I pretend that I'm like water—no colour at all. 'Can't hurt me if he can't see me.' That's what I used to think about Dad. Same went for that William Freeman fella. My grandfather. True enough there are things I want to tell you about him. Things not even Mum knew. But I can't tell you right now. Secrets like those have to be unwrapped at just the right time.

I look inside the Red River Hotel. Pokie lights are still blinking their happy times bright rainbow. They don't sleep. Pat catches me looking at him and flicks his eyes back to the road ahead. I roll down the window and listen to the gravel crunching under the tyres. Let the sound massage my ears. When Mum was here I never thought about what this town was made of. But after the fall, the world shattered into a thousand pieces. Then I realised those little particles of dust floating through the air were a part of every word we said, every breath and step we took. When they float away there'll be nothing left and now this place is all but gone.

2

God-knocking box

I'd only ever passed by Hutchins Road on the school bus. Every other day it's just where the police hide at the bend hoping to nab someone for speeding. But on the day of the funeral, Hutchins Road was a punch in the guts and a ten-car procession.

Pat puts the clicker on and we turn down the road. Can't leave town without paying respects. The sun falls over Pat's eyes and for a moment it looks like they've turned from blue to green. It's only a quarter after eight but the heat is already on. Crickets drone like a one-note symphony. The air feels stretched, and you think about which way you'd run if a fire ripped through. Pat's been here before, buried his mum and dad two weeks apart. Some people are so connected their hearts beat in synchronicity. When one goes, the other can't survive.

'I'll get onto it. Next pay packet, promise.'

There's not even a wooden cross like some of the other new graves have. I wanted Mum's to read *Tell me when it's time to wake up* because she always slept through the alarm. I'd get the porridge on and tell her when breakfast was ready. But Pat said you couldn't write a joke on a headstone.

I can still see the holes in the ground where the fold-up chairs were. They didn't want any of the oldies keeling over with heatstroke. One funeral at a time, Margie said.

At the funeral it was mostly Pat's friends who I didn't know. Men in mismatching suits with chunky black sneakers. Narelle, the Red River barmaid, wore a tight red skirt and strappy heels. She came long after Mum had stopped working at the pub, but maybe it was a solidarity thing. Like she was representing the union for pretty girls behind the bar. I thought the church was supposed to love everyone no matter what you wore but Margie whispered in my ear that it was blasphemous to dress like a hooker in the company of a priest. 'Cheap and nasty spoils the party.'

Margie said I could still come over whenever I wanted and have Monte Carlo biscuits with Cottee's orange cordial. Margie stroked my face and said she could give me jobs for pocket money now. That I could clip her nails and pick up the dog poo her neighbour's terrier Anzac kept leaving under her roses. The veins in her hand ran across the surface of her skin like a kid had drawn on her with blue texta. A map with mountains and tracks that grew deeper every year. They felt nice to touch.

Mrs Hall from school came to the funeral. When she saw me her mouth opened to speak but then she just smiled with one side of her mouth. I also saw Allen and his mum. He gave me a handmade card. There was a lobster on it because that's what he likes to draw at the moment. Its claws were holding a heart. Even Tammy who always calls me a retard was there. She sat at the very back and didn't look at me once, just kept chewing the inside of her cheek like she was trying to whistle.

If you wanted to, you could go and have a look at Mum in her coffin. Her face was so beautiful. The lady in a funny hat who worked there said she would be in an endless sleep and wasn't that a nice place to be. I wanted to say not if your mouth was covered in dirt and worms were turning you into compost. But I just touched her face softly and sang 'Bonnie and Clyde' by Serge. It wasn't the same because there are two parts to the song. Pat said it was time to start so I kissed her on top of the head and blew over her eyes. The priest said some nice things about Mum. That no greater gift was she given than me.

He said it was sad that none of her family could come from France, but I know Mum left when she realised there was no one to stay for. Her own mother thought only of herself, and her brother René had stolen the inheritance, but Mum didn't talk about money because that was vulgar. When the organ music played 'Ave Maria', Pat started to cry in that man kind of way: shoulders all shaking with silent sobs. Margie gave him one of her hankies with the roses sewed onto it. And before I knew it, I was swaying back and forth.

Sometimes things are so sad you just have to sway it out, like you're giving yourself a lullaby. Margie's niece said she knew how I felt, but she didn't. The pounding behind my ears was a tidal wave of furious white noise, pushing me out of the pew and straight into that box. The one in the far-left corner of the church that looks like a wardrobe. Even though I was *in* the church I was not *of* the church because I was never baptised. Still, I just needed a dark space of my own. And if the man upstairs had a problem with that he could knock on the door and tell me himself.

The priest's voice became muffled, which was just fine because I didn't want to hear his words anymore. There were other things I could hear if I closed my eyes real tight and let my ears off the leash. Margie's stomach gurgling. Tammy's eyes trying to blink away tears she did not see coming. Allen moving his neck from side to side—the crunching sound it made because he sleeps on a pillow that is too high for his head. After the organ started playing again and people sang another song about lambs and blessed be thy name, Pat came over and told me to come out because they were going to put Mum in the ground. God never knocked on that box, not even once.

In the ground there's not just *less* time, there's no time. No meetings that run late or birthday parties you were early for, no twiddling of thumbs or chasing the last bus home. You will never think about the past or the future and right now is always. Pat gave me some roses to throw into the grave but I dropped some potatoes down instead. We used to dig up Dutch creams and kipflers, boil them, spread a knife full of butter down the middle and pile on the salt. I smiled at that memory even though it didn't seem right, standing over the top of my dead mother. I wanted to jump in and lie down with her—just one more time.

That was eleven days ago and here we are again like it was yesterday. I wanted to get fake orchids because we wouldn't be back for a while and they would last a lifetime, but Pat said that was crass. So we got yellow petunias from the petrol station. They were a few days old and already starting to droop. I put them down where I thought her arms might be, one bunch in each hand. Pat's silhouette moved so close to mine we merged into one big shadow, large and wide. When death has come and gone some people say 'How can I keep going?' Even when friends bring a beef casserole, do the ironing and gossip about poor Shirley and Geoff who got food poisoning in Bali, that person just can't start again. One day they lie down for a nap while the 5 pm news is on the radio, and they die too.

'Pat, who am I now?' When life mucks you about, sometimes it's hard to know.

'You're the same always…same as…before,' he says with eyes to the ground. But that was a lie. Dirt talkin' is always a lie.

'Am I still real? Do you see me?' Here in this moment I'm losing it all: my words, this place, the past.

Pat's hand reaches out but stops before he can touch my cheek. Maybe I've just gone and disappeared. How could I be real without Mum? When the world was too noisy, she would put a finger to her lips and slow it all down. Taught the wind how to hold its breath. Now everything is sliding backwards and I want to throw up. I leg it through the cemetery, run halfway across the normal Christians, through the Jews and Greek Orthodox. Keep going past the heathens who shouldn't have been there at all, and only stop when I see the tiny crosses. There are headstones too, some with pictures of those babies before they became angels. Why does God gift them to Earth only to snatch them back so quick? I am angry for all of us left behind. God is a selfish man and grief makes you unwhole. My dad once said he would punch Jesus in the face if he had the nerve to come back another time.

I look up into the cloudless sky. 'Make me real!' I scream.

Pat's arms wrap tight around me. I try to get out but he won't let go and after a while I don't want him to. I wonder if those angel babies can still hear their parents whispering—wishing, hoping, praying they'll come back. I wonder if those babies blow birthday kisses to their brothers and sisters; watching as they get older even though angels never can. I wonder if they are watching me right now, telling me it is okay to go and find Mum's spirit.

And do you know what? I stare into that picture of two-year-old Therese Boylan with the rosy cheeks and the curly mop of blonde hair and I hear her say: 'Be it metal or wood, go find the boat.' I think Pat hears it too because he turns to me and nods.

'Let's go.'

3

Hand in hand

We're driving back through town and a semi hurtles past taking up more than its fair share of the road. It's so long it might as well have been a train. The line through Beyen stopped years ago when people forgot what there was to see so far out. The town is slowly waking up now. I see the corner shop with Tran sweeping dust back and forth on the footpath. Alan taking his pug Jojo for a poo, back legs quivering so much she might fall over with the strain. There's Mr Reeler the-hands-on-feeler sitting on a bench in Cullen Park, three-piece St Vinnies grey suit and no socks. People keep throwing bricks into his window 'cause he's a nasty piece of work and isn't allowed into the public swimming pool.

We pass by Miriam's spicy chicken and chips take-away where we had dinner the night before. Jesus had a last supper. People in jail in America also get a special meal before they die. This one lady who buried all her ex-husbands in the backyard, she ate some cornbread, beans and rice, McDonalds Big Mac meal deal, a chocolate milkshake, and cherry vanilla ice-cream with hot apple pie. It's not good to sleep on such a full stomach. Even if you're gonna wake up in hell.

My last meal was eight chicken nuggets, chips and gravy. I drank a sip of Pat's beer and he said my face looked like a ferret's fart. When we laughed some beer came out of my nose and we laughed some more. Good times like that are rare with me and Pat. Almost endangered. I'd been sleeping at his place for the past few nights on account of my house being totally empty. Salvos van had come and gone and I was living out of a suitcase. I saw Mrs Lupido riding down the street in Mum's favourite summer dress. I just can't scratch that memory out of my eyes.

It's never easy to sleep at the beginning of the end. My last night in Beyen was an oven-hot scorcher. Every time I heard a bump outside I reckoned it was a possum keeling over 'cause they can't take their fur coats off. And even though it couldn't be true I swear I heard a train in the distance. *Thumpety thumpety thump.* In my dream I crawled out of bed and flew into the tree outside. There were no clouds to scare me or make me fall. Just a purple-blue night where bats flew across the full moon. I watched myself as I got onto that train, turned around and waved goodbye. If I am going, then who is left behind? The train was so small in the distance now it looked like a toy. That girl—me, myself—she'd gone. Running as far away from her dirty blackness as she could. Only trouble is, wherever you go, there you are.

Making our way down the main drag I see no one's bothered to organise a ticker-tape parade. Doesn't seem proper to leave with no fanfare at all. When we turn onto Harmony Street I see the town statue, that big old metal hand with its palm facing towards me, and it's saying STOP! WAIT! STAY! I grab hold of the steering wheel and we screech to a halt in the middle of the road.

'What-the-hellsmatta-with-ya??!!' Pat clutches his chest like his heart's trying to escape.

'It's a sign!'

'It's not a sign, it's just a big bloody hand!'

Well that wasn't true. It was the BIGGEST hand in the southern hemisphere, made in honour of the town's founder. Lambert Beyen was from Antwerp, which is a town in Belgium. And Belgium is a little country that was swallowed up by other countries fighting around it until someone said, 'Okay let's find a king and draw lines in the dirt and put up stop signs and make this our own place.' So they did and then Belgium became a real country on the map. There used to be a giant called Antigoon who lived by the river in Antwerp. If you wanted to cross you had to give him all your pocket money otherwise he would cut your hand clean off! Then a Roman warrior came and cut off the giant's own hand and threw it in the river. There's a statue of him right in front of the town hall. You can buy little chocolate hands in Antwerp to eat. I thought that sounded nice, but Mum said it was awful because it was from another story about the Belgian king who used to cut real people's hands off in the Congo. She said the Belgians hadn't fully 'reconciled their pasts'. Like going to Pizza Hut, chucking everyone out, eating all the food and then leaving without paying for your meal.

The first hand statue they made in Beyen was moulded from plastic, and in the heat wave of 1986 the fingers melted and it looked like a really old person with arthritis. People started touching the sticky surface and covering it in heaps of fingerprints. So then they had to cart it away because they said someone could actually get hurt for real and that would be a *liability* and the town could not afford to get sued again after that truck accident where Mrs Harrison got run over by a breakaway pack of squealing pigs. If she'd been quick enough she would have nabbed one for her husband Gerald. He's Gary's twin brother, the other butcher in town. So we got a new hand made out of metal. It still gets really hot in summer but no one gets stuck to it. *Het is echt een mooie hand.* If you lived in Antwerp that's how you'd say 'It's a real beauty'.

'Me and Mum used to sit in that hand,' I tell Pat. 'We used to pretend it was taking us for a ride.' Sometimes it still feels like I'm holding on. Pat clears his throat and taps the steering wheel. Then he says real quiet, 'That was a long time ago.'

I stretch my hand out on the window glass. If I close one eye it fits right inside the statue. The engine kicks over again and vibrations run up my fingers. Pat was right. The hand wasn't telling me to stop. It was pushing me away. I look in the rear-view mirror as it gets smaller and smaller. My backpack sits on my lap. I unzip it slowly. I let my fingers run over the few precious things I was allowed to take with me. My proper good fork, the only one in the southern hemisphere that does not leave too much metal in your mouth. Mum's fancy necklace, a perfect circle of rainbow moonstones that used to be her mum's. I had to take it because it's an air loom, which is something precious that passes down from one generation to the next. Mum used to wear it even if it wasn't a special occasion. When she wanted to make a boring job fancy she'd whip it on and peel those potatoes like a princess. I don't like having things around my neck so I've brought it but I won't wear it. There are other things that would be easier to leave behind, but I *have* to keep, like a fish and a snow globe.

Mum and Dad were never meant to be. Light and shadow, soft and sharp, lost and found. Me in the middle like a chook with its head cut off, going round and round in circles. I don't really feel whole or a pretty sum of my parts. Not the right sum at least. Imagine this: a shiny fishing lure lying in the middle of a dirt puddle all the way out here in whoop de whoop. The hooks had come off, rusted and bent out of shape. Can't get further from the sea than here. This tiny metal fish of mine is the story of Dad. I was running away from him when I found it. Put my headphones on and tried to cancel out his shouting, but I could still see tiny specks of spit and angry vowels flying out of his mouth. Beautiful silver scales so small and perfect, each half-moon laid over the next. I picked that fish up and ran my fingers across every one. Every stroke, every scale shimmering in the sun. Reminded me to breathe all the way to the bottom of my lungs. I kept that fish in my pocket and when things got too loud, nothin' left but to run, I'd hold it between my fingers. Count the scales until all was said and done.

The snow globe is the story of Mum. Inside that perfectly round glass dome is Paris. Actually it's just the Eiffel Tower but if you shake it up snowflakes float all around, then fall slowly to the bottom. Mum gave it to me. She found it in the cat-rescue op shop in Wyndful Gully that one summer we went on a holiday. Well camping, 'cause we couldn't afford to go anywhere but the next town across. We walked there. All the kids at the camp site had a go shaking the globe as hard as they could, timing how long the snow took to settle. Twenty-seven seconds was the longest. It's the only time I had something everyone else wanted. Until someone's dad took kids for a ride in the back of his ute, doing donuts and crazy stuff. Mum wouldn't let me go and I was glad because one boy called Conor fell out and broke his arm. The night before Mum went for good we set a new record. Sat nose to nose on each side of that globe until the last snowflake dropped. Thirty-three seconds. When we looked up I saw myself in her eyes, reflected a thousand times over like a picture in a picture. That's called an optical illusion because there's only one of me, and now there's none of her.

I've also brought a photo of me and Mum sitting in the Beyen hand. A reporter from the *Dry Gully Gazette* took it when the statue was unveiled. We're high-fiving each other and smiling so hard our cheeks look shiny. The photo didn't make it into the gazette, but the reporter sent us a copy anyway.

Pat doesn't go around potholes, he goes straight through them at full speed, and my bum clears the seat for a moment. I take the snow globe out of my bag. The rising sun reflects off the plastic dome and sends a piercing light into my eyes. I can still see Mum's finger-prints on the side.

A bit of my heart catches on Mrs Devlin's splintered fence at the end of Baker Street, trying to hold on even though nothing can ever be the same again. Because I killed my mum.

4

Clouds moving too fast

We've only been on the road for six kilometres so maybe I shouldn't have told you that yet. Now you're probably rippin' all the pages out of this story and throwing them into the fire. Watching the words curl into themselves and float away. Please don't go, not yet. Pat's just about the worst travelling companion there is, so I need some extra company. When I close my eyes I'm under the waves, trying to come up to the surface but then I suddenly hit my head on the bottom of the ocean. No way up and out of something like this. If there was a God I'd be asking how he could've let me do what I did. Then again, you don't have to be a bad person to do bad things. Half the people in jail say they didn't mean to do it, that it was just a misunderstanding.

Right now Classic Cougar 97.3 FM is playing eight from the eighties and, without even realising it, Pat's tapping along to *A-ha*. He's popped a piece of gum and

I think his ticker's calmed down. Me and Pat have never talked about what happened. Men drink and punch their way through feelings. That's what Dr. Juno Nova Martinez said on *Oprah*.

Even though we had to leave everything behind memories will still hitch a ride. Maybe if there'd been breaking news on the radio forecasting 'a terrible day for terrible things to happen' then obviously we would have stayed put. But it was beautiful weather with no clouds at all. Not a single one.

Every Sunday we went to Margie's place so Mum could give her a mani/pedi because Margie's back might break if she tried to touch her toes. Her spinal cord was hollowed out and dry. Mum would put all the nail clippings in a sandwich bag because Margie said they reassured her. 'Can't keel over if the hair is flowing and the nails are growing.'

We saw a lot of seniors, me and Mum. Everyone can look radiant if they know what their colour system is and attend to their roots on a regular basis. The oldies at the *Best Intentions Nursing Home* all liked Tina Arena. 'She's come so far,' they'd say and pass the *Woman's Day* mag back and forth. Tina's big in France. She made Mum wistful.

Before we left for Margie's that day I'd dug up some potatoes for her Irish stew. I loved shaking in the

Worcestershire sauce, watching all the little circles of oil float on the top and sucking out the marrow. *Parfait.* Digging up spuds was a game for me and Mum. We'd race 'em down the driveway; Mum gave them names and everything.

'Spudtacular comes round the bend with Alligator-tater close behind. Mish-mash makes a last go of it, but it's Spudtacular who comes away with a strong win!'

Margie's house is right across the road from the bus stop on the corner of Canon Street. She'd made me some pikelets for morning tea and that day I chose strawberry jam with cream. Mum got to work on Margie's toenails, so I went outside and ran my fingertips along the rose bushes. Margie says they're like the pretty girls at her school: nice to look at but prickly as all hell.

Then I heard something. Scratch and scrabble, twist and turn as the baby birds wriggled closer to one another. They were in one of the big gum trees on the other side of the fence. The shadows came. Moved across the paddock like ghost horses that used to run wild across the fields when no one lived here at all. They came fast those shadows. I looked up and saw dark clouds swirling. Now, don't get me wrong, clouds are usually good because they hold the rain. But magic is a powerful thing. Sometimes it can turn the world upside down.

The baby birds were crying out loud. Hungry squawking babies calling for their mama to feed them.

And I was scared they'd be lost in the storm, that the winds might tear their nest apart and send them flying. As I climbed the tree I could hear Mum's voice travelling on the wind. I saw her in the distance out by Margie's back door. Her hair was whipping round her face and she had to hold it back with one hand.

'Dylan...DYLAN!'

I felt her fear whooshing out like a flood, rising up and filling my lungs. But it was too late to do anything so I just held on. Mum started to climb the tree and my eyes locked with hers through the howling wind and the booming thunder. I looked up to the sky, begging the clouds to stop.

In that flash of a second I took my eyes off Mum and she fell. The branch broke clean away and she went back towards the ground before I could scream, 'Wait, sorry clouds, don't hurt my mum, I was the one who made you angry! Throw me into the sky and toss me round like a ragdoll, but leave Mum alone!' In slow motion my arm reached out to hers and hers to mine.

As soon as she hit the ground the wind stopped blowing, the clouds floated away and the birds stopped their crying. Stillness bleeding through my ears. Margie standing by the porch, one hand leaning on the wall and the other on her bad hip. She didn't want to move, didn't want to see what had happened. I slid down the tree, fingers peeling off the bark in big strips as I went.

Thud, I hit the ground, scrambled over to Mum. Her left leg was bent back the wrong kind of way. I brushed a strand of hair out of her face. How could she look so lovely and be dead at the same time? I tried to breathe life back into Mum. I pumped her chest, but beyond those beautiful glassy eyes everything was broken. A plague of cicadas was trapped in my head, a pounding drone. I wanted to run through the fields away from it all, back to the house where Mum was still humming to Serge Gainsbourg or calling that potato race.

When that police lady came she tried to pull my fingers back off Mum's arm, but I growled at her so loud it scared me too. Cars arrived and lots of people moved about, but all I could understand was Margie saying, 'I don't know, I don't know. I need to sit down. Oh, my Lord.'

The police lady sat by my side the whole time and talked softly. She wouldn't let anyone else near me until the sun had set and a whisper on the wind told me it was time to go. It was getting cold and the heat from Mum had gone. I could feel all these eyes watching when I went with that police lady. She had to help me walk because I felt so tired and weak and I didn't even care that I'd peed my pants.

There were so many men and I didn't know any of them. Some had police uniforms and others wore a shirt and tie. Some of them talked to the police lady quietly but none of them would look at me. They turned their faces away or pretended to read something on a clipboard. There was a big white sheet that someone was holding and I knew they were going to put it over Mum, but I didn't want to see that. I didn't want to see her disappear. I felt raw and cold—a back-door draught shooting up my back.

We went through the house and Margie was sitting at the kitchen table with a hand over her mouth. She reached out to me but accidentally knocked over her cold cup of tea.

I went in a police car. That is something I'd always wanted to do but it did not feel exciting. People in the street were staring at me. I could feel their eyes burning into the back of my head. I waited for Mum to walk into the living room but everything was already beginning to vanish. The last time she stood by the back steps to catch a break in the weather. The last time she sat on the couch and braided my hair while we watched *Ghostbusters* on TV. The last time she was in bed and let me lie next to her. When we were comrades against the world. So much emptiness it made me want to hide in the wardrobe and wait for the darkness that had taken her to take me too.

The police lady said that Pat was coming and she gave me lemonade, which was warm so I didn't drink it. We just sat at the table and she kept asking me what had happened, but I didn't open my mouth in case a scream came out and never stopped. Then Pat's headlights flooded the room. My heart was beating so fast because I wanted him to help me, but I had broken Mum myself, and she had gone away from him too. I looked out the window and two policemen had to hold him back, trying to calm him down because he had a little pink bottle and said that everything was all right, that they were wrong, he had Mum's favourite perfume and it was all okay now. The police didn't know Mum and Pat had had a fight and he was trying to make it right again.

My gut sank like a stone in the river because I knew that Pat would punish me for this. If I had more discipline, I would not have looked away from Mum and let her fall. Nothing truer than that. So I ran into that wardrobe. Inside I listened to them all talking until there was nothing left to say and the police cars had gone and Pat had stopped walking back and forth over creaking floorboards and the night finally took the noise. But the dark did not take my pain or Pat's. Only hid it until the morning came. You wake up with a start and remember what sleep had let you forget.

When I went to the loo early the next morning I watched Pat curled up on the couch holding the bottle of perfume he had bought Mum. *Anais Anais*. During the night his dreams had made him small. They don't disappear you know; dreams and memories will float out of your head and go through other folk. And I walked right through one of Pat's memories in that moment. He was sitting at the pokie machine, watching Mum behind the bar. Made a bet with himself that if triple cherries came up he'd ask her out. He can still see them falling into place: 1, 2, 3. The pokie machines are his kind of magic and they've brought her to him. He looks up, and Mum's smiling. She already knows.

Back in the living room I can see Pat's pillow wet with tears. I want to hold Pat and share my sadness, but if I wake him up, everything will break again. I saw a painting once in a gallery. Mum stared at it forever. A sheep is crying in the snow and her baby lamb is dead on the ground. No one can help her and she is alone.

5

Never-knowing

That morning Pat sat in the kitchen still as a statue. I hovered by the door but didn't open my mouth in case I accidentally screamed just to break the silence. Then he shoved a chair out from the table.

'Eat.'

And so I did. But my cornflakes were disturbingly loud and Pat didn't talk to me for the rest of breakfast. When he put my bowl in the sink he turned around and said, 'What happened?' So I told him about the clouds but he just shook his head and said, 'No, no, no, no. No!' Clasped his hands together and said I shouldn't have been up the tree, if only I hadn't climbed the bloody tree. I didn't know if he was praying or was gonna hit me so I put my boxer hands up just in case. Pat was the one who looked scared, like I'd just appeared out of nowhere. When he moved towards me I ducked to the left and ran out of the room.

Hid in the wardrobe for the rest of the day and counted to 100 again and again and again. Mathematics is a discipline that keeps everything in line. At 7.47 pm my little sparrow friend came to visit. He only has one foot so I knew it was him. That's what happens when someone dies, people come to pay their respects. He watched as I made and ate my grilled cheese sandwich that was not grilled. Put his head to the side like he was saying, 'Just watch me. I am light and bouncy.' As I ate my night-time lunch I laughed and said, 'Hey, Mum, he's back!' Then everything slid away like a wave rolling back into the sea. I called it the never-knowing: when your mind pretends it's never known that awful thing ever happened. There was another kind of never-knowing, which was all to do with Pat and his phone calls. He said he was making arrangements that DID NOT CONCERN ME but I was very concerned indeed. When people mumble on the phone I am always concerned because sometimes the next day things have changed for good.

On the fifth night Pat came into my room and sat on the bed then walked around, pulled the curtains shut and sat on the bed again. He said the funeral was in the morning so I should pick out a pretty dress to wear because we were saying goodbye to Mum. I said, 'Where will we be?' And Pat said, 'Well…we'll still be here. You'll be…' He stopped and looked up like he was counting cracks in the ceiling. 'I got a lotta things to do and I can't do more than that, you know?'

Even though I didn't know, I nodded my head because I think that was the answer he wanted. One without words.

The night before we buried her I had a dream Mum was the one stuck up the tree and I had to rescue *her*. I couldn't climb up because the tide was coming in. Water swirling around my feet with a sea swallowing me slowly, creeping higher and higher. Then the whole tree lifted out of the ground, roots ripping and tearing like a tooth extraction. The tree just whooshed up into the air and blew away light as a feather.

At the bottom of the hole was my snow globe. I knew that if I went into the hole I might never come out again but I had to get it so I put one foot in and stumbled down, dirt going into my mouth and under my nails as I tried to hold onto the side, but I just kept slipping as the hole got deeper and deeper until the sky disappeared. A rumbling avalanche of brown snow fell on top of me. I screamed and screamed but no one could hear. Then Pat was shaking me awake. Sometimes dreams bring messages about what you have to do in your real life. And I knew that Mum was telling me she still had to get back home and it was my duty to navigate her spirit across the sea to Paris. I just had to find where the boat and her spirit were.

I felt sick all through the funeral. Pat had put Mum in the dress she'd worn when they first met. Made it all about him, and I felt thunder in my chest. Death is like the last glass of milk when there is no more in the fridge and the shop is closed 'cause it's late Sunday arvo. When Mum went in the ground she should have been in something timeless but Pat said it was too late. I told him there'd be a royal commission and he'd be called as a witness. Pat apologised, but I said life was about *deeds not words* and told him to put it in the bank for safekeeping because I did not want to cash his sorry cheque right now. Then I walked into Mum's room and folded her silk scarves. They were thin just like paperbark. I wrapped them all around, covering myself in swirly softness of light and colour. I was a butterfly. New and fresh from my chrysalis. Why do pretty things die so quickly?

6

Barry

'All right, keep ya shoppin' list in ya head.'

Now I'm back in the car. On the road with Pat. I've been talking to myself with the mute button on. For how long, I wonder? Memories drag you into the past whenever they like—I wish Pat knew that. He winces and shakes his head at me.

'It's a bloody distraction all that whisper talkin'.'

I look out the dirty window; the freckles of dust look like a science riddle only Stephen Hawking could solve. And then I'm thinking about time again. Wish I could chuck all the hours left down a black hole. I want to be far away from the stinking heat and bloody blowflies, rattled nerves and desperate times where everyone is parched. Waiting for something to break, turn, shift and come good again. Out here this land is endlessly unforgiving. You think you can put a road through it and make it your own, but the bush will swallow you up whole if you get too cocky. It takes people in until they're too deep to be found. I've been in their dreams too. Stumbling over rocks and caked in red dust. Following a dry riverbed to a sea they'll never find.

Sometimes I think Pat would like to disappear that way too. You see, that was the fight he had with Mum the night before she died. He didn't want to go anywhere, especially not with me. But Mum always said we were a package deal and if he wanted to be with her, he had to learn how to love me too. The whole world was waiting for us if we stuck together. In Paris we'd eat chocolate éclairs at the top of the tower. Count the people below, dressed in their Sunday best even on a Tuesday, scuttling about being important and mysterious. Or watch the cafe tables on the footpath, where people blow smoke into each other's faces and whisper secrets. No one would know I was black 'cause I'd speak their language too.

Pat sure was surprised when those strangers with sweaty armpits came knocking on the front door a couple of days after Mum died. Thought they were God-botherers at first.

'We're sorry for your loss.' The lady spoke so slow I thought there must have been something wrong with her.

44

'Don't do that, pretend like you know,' Pat says with his right leg jiggling up and down under the table. I had to go outside and play while they 'discussed matters'. That's what adults say when they want to talk about the things you have done. Or what will be done. *For your own good.*

When they were leaving the woman crinkled her eyes at me and talked real slow again like I was deaf. 'You're a very brave girl.'

Pat made a lot of phone calls after that. I can tell you now, that wolf inside me knew what he was up to. It whispered soft enough so only I could hear: 'Remember to forget kid, remember to forget. Now is not the time for unspoken truths.' He was right. I didn't want to know what was down the road, around the corner, where my ever after would be and who I might turn into once I got there. I worry about the things I don't know yet. Surprises aren't always fun. Like a birthday party no one comes to. Or when you find your dad asleep on the footpath one afternoon holding his own front tooth in his hand. To avoid any surprises like that I didn't ask who Pat was talking to on the phone. I just decided to stick with the plan I'd made with Mum. Pat didn't believe she had a spirit. Said God and the after-life was a con for people too weak to see life for what it really was.

•

'I gotta…shake the snake,' Pat says and pulls over. I watch as he slides down the embankment like he's being swallowed by quicksand. There's nothing in the car to eat except a bag of jubes. I pick all the yellow ones out and throw them into my mouth. The jelly sinks into the ridges of my back teeth and my tongue flicks them out again. I watch the gum trees watching me and wonder if they know of Barry back home. When all the noise got too much like Dad screaming and throwing things, Mum would say 'Go visit Barry,' and I'd run down to the paddock at the bottom of Novis Lane where that big old gum tree stood. Ran so hard I'd be bent over when I got there, lungs sucking in more air than they could let out. Tall dry grass tickling the hairs on my legs. I'd climb into the cave in the base of Barry's trunk.

Once when I was hiding inside Barry, I found myself in one of Dad's old memories. My grandmother is crying and little-boy Dad wants to help but doesn't know how. He watches as the pills fall like rainbow candy into her hand. When she stops crying and lies down on the bed, he stays with her for the rest of the day. Stroking her hair. Holding her hand. Until his older sister comes home from school. She pulls him off the bed; tells him to let Mama sleep. They want to pretend for as long as possible that she might wake up. And he will always remember looking back at his mama before the door closes, the palm of one hand turned upwards. Her fingers spread out delicately like a fan calling him back with a silent request: 'Wait, don't go.'

I knew that moment. I knew that hand. You are never further away from yourself than when your mama has gone. Dead mothers are the worst legacy of all. But you cannot keep that pain in your fists and take it out on other people. Sometimes when I curled up inside Barry I thought of being a cicada in the ground. I'm not alive yet and all I can do is wait until it's time to dig my way up to the surface. All the noises are covered in a blanket of dirt and have no sharp edges at all. Inside Barry, time is always somewhere else and I don't remember how long I've been there until Mum comes and finds me. She tries to hide the bruises but her smile is always a bit broken. I just hold her hand and walk extra slow through the paddocks because I want this to be forever, just the two of us.

Out here with Pat in the middle of nowhere, I wonder if all these other gum trees are safekeeping secrets too. Maybe there are stories deep down inside the roots or buried between layers of bark. Like the letters I hid inside Barry. I didn't write them and they weren't written for me. But I reckon when Dad left for good, he hoped I would find them all the same. Men always keep things they reckon will come in handy down the track. But that track is long and full of spare parts collecting not much

47

more than dust. Dad was like Pat that way. The shed out back was full of junk from his hard-rubbish runs. Before the council truck chugged around town he would cruise the streets looking for treasure. Said people chucked good things out so they had an excuse to buy something shiny and new. I often hid in that shed, playing hide and seek with Mum.

One day I hid behind the bonnet of an old rusted Holden ute propped up against the back wall. Maybe it had been there when we moved in; I can't remember. Underneath was a metal cabinet. And inside the middle draw was a shoebox stuffed with letters. 'From Michael' was scrawled in kid writing at the bottom of every single one. That's my dad's name. I stayed crouched behind the bonnet and read those letters over and over again. Forgot about the game I'd been playing, until I heard Mum screaming my name. Then my heart beat me back into the real world. Shoved the letters into my sock and stumbled out of the shed. Mum was mad as hell; thought someone had stolen me away. The next morning I ran straight down to Barry and hid those letters, carved out a slit in his trunk just wide enough to shove them inside. A bark pocket for past wishes and woes.

Pat's taking his sweet time shaking the snake, so I slide my fingers into the bottom of my backpack and pull that stash of letters out. I'd marked them all with numbers so I could keep the story in the right order, but in the end it didn't seem to matter. Dad's trying his best to stay on the lines but his thoughts travel faster than his hand can scribble. He asks, 'Are you coming back? Do you still love me?' He wonders how it is possible to walk home from school one day and find every single piece of his father gone. No coat on the hook or whistle in the hallway. Just footprints leading out the door—to where, why, how?

He's too scared to send those words in case the answer, the only answer, is 'No'. So he writes the same letter over and over again. But without an answer, questions buzz around his head like TV static. Finally the noise ignites a volcano in his mind and it grows and grows as he does, from a lonely little boy into a man who likes to be alone. A man who hurts other people like he wanted to hurt his dad. Finally he leaves his family too. How could he not? It was in his genes. I trace the words on the page with my fingers; the question mark is like a snake with a full stop at the bottom. If you asked, I'd still say I don't know why I keep those letters so long past their due date. But the wolf inside would shake his head and call me a liar. He knows as well as I do they need to be delivered, one way or another.

Sitting here in the hot car my mind's playing silly buggers. Maybe there are real snakes out there and Pat's been bitten by a black one with a red belly. Maybe that snake is coming for me. I've left all the car doors wide open, so I close them again, catching my little finger in the last one as I slam it shut. Throbbing like a drum it feels like it's gone puffed up triple size, even though it looks the same. I scream blue murder and Pat comes stumbling over the dunes, pants halfway down his legs. A thin line of blood runs across the inside of my nail.

Now a scratch is okay—you've got enough time to tell the blood to go back the way it came. But if I get cut from a tin lid or a blood vessel bursts 'cause I blew my nose too hard then there's no telling what might happen. Maybe I'd go all haemophiliac and keel over right there. And even though it is right and normal to have your 'little friend' visit every month, a period is not friendly and when it finally comes it could be the end of me if the bloody tap isn't turned off in time. Besides, there's magic water in your blood that keeps you alive. If it leaks out, you're very quickly not.

'What the hell are you screechin' about?' Pat's furrowed brow is all shiny with sweat, bulging on his forehead like a fleshy avalanche. No one's pretty when they're cross. He looks at my finger.

'You're not bloody Rasputin all right, you're not gonna die. It's not even on the surface!'

I still get the first-aid kit out and plaster my finger with three bandaids so I don't have to see the blood under my nail. I try to stretch out those creases on Pat's forehead with my good hand, but he just slaps it away.

'Just lay off, all right! You're drivin' me round the bend!'

'I'm not driving anywhere! It's not my fault you've got a weak bladder!'

He starts the car up, clears his throat like he's coughing up half a lung and we hit the road again.

'Rasputin never had no problems with his blood. It was that boy prince,' I tell Pat just to set the record straight.

He sniffs through his nose and I squish a smile between my lips. Cat-bum style.

7

He's right on time, that Pat O'Brien

After a while you forget how long you've been driving. The road becomes a no-man's-land that stretches on forever. I wake up with a jolt, confused. The inside of my thighs are wet with sweat but there's a drought in my head, pounding. I crack open a can of Coke that tastes like warm sugar water. Pat holds out his hand so I pass it over knowing that's that. Men take one gulp and it's gone, Adam's apple bobbin' up and down like a cork in the water. When I shift, knee sweat trickles down my legs. Nothing feels good in this heat and mess makes it worse. The car's full of Pat's work stuff, promotional posters and a cardboard cutout of a guy holding a beer. In his hand there's a slit where Pat puts brochures about a competition to win prizes.

Pat works for a beer company. It's not his job to sell the beer, but to sell the *selling* of the beer. He travels from one dusty town to the next, talking to the publican (the man who runs the pub and might have a wife or might not). Pat has to find out which beer will sell, survive or suck. What the customers want and what they don't know they want, but will as soon as Pat's company gives them a free hat with every carton. He has to tell everyone that it's 'no worries, too easy, not a drama', that he'll 'call that one straight in, sort it out, turn it around, check in, check out and call again soon'. One publican called Tom always popped a coldie on the counter at 12.45 pm, leant on the bar with both hands stretched out. And come rain or shine Pat would walk on in. 'He's right on time, that Pat O'Brien.'

Pat would smile and down that beer in five seconds flat.

After business Pat and the publican have a yarn. This is when two men mumble about the way of the world, the lay of the land and old Farmer Ned who packed up and left Susan to take care of the whole bloody lot. The drought that wiped out half the crop and cattle that had to be shot 'cause you can't let a walking bag of bones suffer like that. Then there's Joan that's on dialysis in the city three times a week so for her birthday the CWA ladies got on a bus and brought the whole bingo hall to her, nurses joined in too. And what about the Thompson boy who just got up one morning, ate his corn flakes, kissed his mum on the cheek, walked into the shed and shot himself with his father's gun. Yeah. A yarn pretty much covers it all.

But I've got things to talk about too. Secrets from the past. I close my eyes and search inside my backpack. Feel the wrinkled texture of creased paper on the tips of my fingers, run circles round and round the page, lines up and across, down and over onto the other side like a wayward map with a million directions. It's a drawing of an eagle flying through the sky with a long neck, blue face, purple eyes and an orange-feathered Mohawk. 'To Michael,' it says. These are the words of my grandfather, William Freeman. The only words of his I have ever seen. The picture is a bit torn and there's a Vegemite stain in the corner. If you look close enough you can see my dad's little-kid fingerprints in those brown smudges. Like ink.

That bird's like me. A bit funny-looking. Not quite right. I remember when Dad gave it to me. He was sitting at the end of my bed. He was crying so I'm pretty sure he was drunk. I waited for him to say something but he just bowed his head down like he was gonna kiss my feet. I thought I'd seen that eagle fly through the night skies in Beyen, wings heavy and tired trying to find somewhere to land. Maybe I just dreamed it. After all, they don't come from here. Hard to tell waking and sleeping lives apart sometimes.

'When was the last time youse went up this way?' Pat asks.

I had been here before, a long time ago. Mum said once we went to visit my grandfather, but I don't remember. He's probably got volcanoes in his head too—I would have gone against my will or written a protest sign on cardboard. That's what French people do. *Resist.* Sometimes I imagined him as a big shadow travelling across the land, sending small creatures running under rocks for cover. He'd scream so loud the earth would shatter into lots of pieces like it used to be and we'd all be floating around on Titanic plates. For the sake of keeping everyone together I tried not to think about him too much. If I were the gambling kind I'd bet he's the reason why Dad went bad. No doubt about it.

'Never been here before,' I say just to play it safe. Pat bangs on the air-conditioner, which never fixes anything.

'Machines are strong on the outside and delicate underneath like a Turkish Delight covered in steel.'

'Yeah, righto. Maybe you should go on *Sale of the Century*. Win us a new air-con unit.'

I crank down the window and the cardboard-cutout man in the back seat almost flies out! I reckon people would love to see him floating overhead holding a beer like he's saying, 'Cheers, good on youse all!' to everyone down below. But Pat shouts at me to roll the window back up again. The plastic handle snaps off which, as the mechanic told Pat, was the car *passively demonstrating its lack of servicing*. Pat just got fixed what he could afford, not what was needed.

'Listen, Dylan. I still got a job to get done. That's what you do in the real world.'

'I'm in the real world too,' I said. But then I started to think about how I would support myself in Paris without a job. I'm only fourteen and don't really have any work experience apart from picking up Margie's toenail clippings and putting them in a plastic sandwich bag. With no sustainable income I'd fall into a spiral of poverty and end up on the streets, standing in line waiting to get a cup of soup from Le Salvation Army. My clothes would turn to shreds and they'd shave my knotty hair off. Hair is an important signifier of identity. If I had no hair how would I remember who I was?

'Don't let them shave my hair, Pat, please!' I cry so hard snot slides down the back of my nose into my mouth. It tastes salty. Pat's got one hand on the wheel as he pulls out a big blue hanky, the one Margie gave him at the funeral. I don't even know if he's washed it since but I take it anyways and bury my whole face inside. I'm breathing through the cloth, watching my mouth blow a hole in and out, in and out. I count until my eyes are quiet and there are no more tears. Pat shoves the cardboard-cutout man under merchandise boxes in the back and tells me to go for glory, crack the window wide open. That's Pat. A frozen river that melts in the middle of winter.

I wind the handle down and this time it doesn't break. Whoosh! I suck in hot blowy air and look out over the paddocks. High, dry grass moving side to side in the wind.

'You got a yarn for me?' says Pat. He glances over but all I see is the wide blue sky reflected back in his sunnies. He gives me the go-ahead with a nod 'cause he knows I got hundreds of them. Stories are everywhere—you just gotta turn on your senses and wait. I hear those blades turning, the big wind machines that birds fly into. They were far away, beyond the mountain range that bordered the horizon. I can hear lots of things that the eyes can't see. So I tell Pat about those machines that store energy in the ground. Wind turns those propellers round and round and then if you were to go underground you would find tunnels where all those blades are turning other little blades and wires and cogs and locks and grooves and pistons and shoots. All working together to put energy into little metal boxes that men come and collect at the end of the day. The light down there is fluorescent electrical blue like threads of lightning, and if you touched it you might go flying down those tunnels so fast you'd end up in Estonia or somewhere else unexpected.

The energy collectors wear special suits and gloves that protect them almost one hundred per cent from all the loose electric particles. Sometimes when they pick up the metal boxes they can still get a little shock, like when you run on the carpet during library time and then sit next to Cole Larsen and touch his arm and you hear that 'crack!' They also wear special glasses because if you look too closely at the energy it makes your eyes go see-through and zaps all the colour out. Then no one would know how to talk to you because eye colour reflects your personality. Brown is warm and open, blue is intolerant and aloof. The energy is then put in trucks that carry it all over the country. Not too many people know they are watching the Friday night footie or cooking spag bol because of those boxes underground.

Pat says the propeller machines are called turbines and if he could, he'd watch them go round all day, until the sun had set and turned them into giant shadow puppets.

8

White vultures

Ahead I can see the outline of a petrol station. There's a coach there too and all the people milling around look like the little dwarfs from *Snow White* marching off to the mines. The gold's long gone from here but they're spoilt for choice if they're after roo nuggets. When I step out of the car and straighten my legs, oh boy my knees feel Gerry-hat-trick. Dropping my head I look between my legs and see the last of the dwarfs heading back towards the bus. Even upside down I can see they're as old as my knees are painful. A whole gaggle of them with high-pitched voices, sun visors and sneakers so white they gotta be straight out of the box. But one of them, I can feel it, has sorrow like a sharp stone in her shoe. Something that lady thought she'd left behind was dragging her down all the same. I could help that woman come up for air; tell her what she needed to hear even if it hurt.

'Now you stay there, righto?' Pat says and he goes inside the petrol station to pay just as his big old clunky phone starts to ring.

Divine intervention—a sign from JC himself. I press a button and hold it to my ear. A man with a voice like gravel answers so maybe it is actually God.

'Are you there yet?' he barks.

The oldies are lining up, ready to board the bus again.

'Almost.'

I hang up, stuff the phone in my pocket and run over. They're all talking at the same time like channel-hopping on the TV.

'…oh, but that's what I told Joe!'

'…she's so surly, pay no mind.'

'…grew over half her neck!'

I follow one thread but get the tale end of another, all the words knotted up like I got crazy voices in my head. And before I know it I'm on that bus sitting in the ninth row on the left-hand side by the window. (Inside the servo Pat's thinking about whether to get a Chiko roll or not. I still got time.) Then this nice-looking lady sits down next to me, but it's not her I'm looking for. She's a human dot-to-dot, hundreds of freckles jumping up and down between her wrinkles. Her name is Lou and she's come from Atlanta, which is where they make Coke for the rest of the world. She says she hadn't seen me at the last pick-up and am I one of the guides for the

Indigenous Reservation? Involving the young people in these tourism ventures she says, is such a positive thing to combat all the problems we have, which their First People have as well. She isn't making much sense but I don't want to embarrass her so I say that yes, this is a working trip and I push some buttons on Pat's phone to make my story look real.

When I look up more of the old ladies have gathered round me in the ninth row. Like these vultures in a cartoon Mum thought was very sad because it showed *how indifferent the west had become to despair that was not its own.* In the cartoon the vultures were standing over this starving African baby. It looked very sick and one of the vultures says, 'Look, it's still moving.' Sometimes there are messages in cartoons that people can read through the pictures, but I am not one of those people.

The ladies on the bus kind of look like vultures because of their craggly skin and wide-open eyes, gaping. But they smile like a hungry grandmother. One of them asks if I could tell a story from the Dreamtime and I don't know which one she means. So I tell her about the last dream that got stuck in my head. I could fly and ran really fast off a cliff, flew over to the shops, got some milk and a can of peas and even though it was not on the list a Violet Crumble which I ate in the shopping line. Then all these ants came and ate the crumbs so I had to run out because they were suddenly huge but then I couldn't fly and my feet felt like lead so I had to leave the peas behind. I went up in the sky again but then crashed down into a paddock and woke up with a really big shock.

The women stare in wonder nodding their heads and Doris says that their First Nations people also had an affinity with nature and animals. Ants aren't animals; they're in a different category, *genus buggus*. I'm scared they might turn into real vultures if I tell them I'm not Aboriginal. But I am browner than some Koori kids 'cause I saw a girl once with blue eyes and blonde hair even though her brothers were all dark. Sometimes when we went to Boyd's Creek, which has two IGA supermarkets one at each end and a drive-through Maccas, I'd be waiting for one of them to look at me and say, 'I know you feel shame, 'cause I feel it too.' Even though sometimes I got called 'sis' or 'tidda' there was nothing underneath my skin that made me one and the same. I still wished and wished for it because maybe then I'd have a sister or brother for real. And thirty-seven relatives called Aunty. Is skin enough to be family? No one's ever set me straight there.

'Tell us more about your...knowing,' Doris said, real low and quiet.

'If I cannot be a singer like Tina Arena I will work with the animals, mostly orangutans which are technically primates so I would be a primatologist.'

Now I feel like *I'm* the monkey. Stuck in a zoo with all these faces staring at me wondering if I'm gonna do a trick. But I keep going because no one ever listens to me. Not like this.

'An *ologist* is someone whose brain is very specific. Mine is. Doctors have said so. I will go to Borneo and look after the baby orangutans that have lost their mothers because we use too much palm oil. They have big eyes and always seem to hunch over like they do not know how to start the day or where they are supposed to be and if they could speak the only thing they would say is "oh well" and then climb very slowly up into a tree and go to sleep.'

Still not a word from the granny brigade. I take the silence as permission to continue, like I'm giving my maiden speech in parliament and everyone has to be quiet even if I'm way boring.

'If I cannot be a primatologist I will be a taxidermist, which is not a dentist who drives around. It is a person that gives dead animals an eternal smile. It is legal to hang them on the wall. If you have a library you can put them on the mantelpiece.'

Then the bus pulls away and I see Pat bolting back to the car, slipping on the gravel. One leg falls from under him and he has to crouch on the ground for a moment to get his balance. That's when he sees me looking through the window of the bus. And three shades of red rise up his neck covering his entire face. 'Right!' he thinks, 'You bloody little ratbag!'

He gets into the car and tyres spin round like he's at a drag race. Then Evelyn asks if I could say something in my native tongue so in French I say: 'Your boobs are falling down.' I shouldn't have said that even though it is true. When you are old everything starts to head south like a runny egg cut with the wrong knife and there is very little you can do about it. Margie says everyone's tits and bits end up dropping, dragging or drooping. 'Surrender now!' she used to say when she drank sherry with Mum. But it doesn't seem to matter in this case because the ladies just look at each other like I've told them a little secret and aren't they lucky to have heard it.

Then we all hear loud beeping and look out the back window. There is Pat holding his hand on the horn with wide eyes goggling at me. He pulls up alongside the driver and points. Everyone is on one side of the bus and I wonder if we might topple over. Bob up the front says to Walter, 'Hey, maybe it's one of them Mad Max fellas!'

The bus pulls over, Pat storms on and pulls me out. All the ladies get really worked up and say, 'Where are you taking her?' Pat says, 'She doesn't belong here.' Doris gets all huffy: 'Well, where does she belong? This is all her land, *we* are the visitors!' I tell Doris it is okay, that my land used to be 44 Carroll Street, Beyen. Not this highway in the middle of nowhere.

And then I see the woman I came to find, two rows down and over. Much smaller than me, drawn back into herself, she was. I feel her bruised heart so I whisper in her ear: 'She can still run in her sleep.' Other people's stories thunder through me like a bolting horse but before I can pull the reins in and get a good look, the pictures in my head have galloped off for good. So when Walter asks how I know her granddaughter was hit and run over by that drugged-up Latino fella so high he might've been on Mount Everest, I can't answer. But I do know that in that girl's dreams her back is not broken and at the farmhouse she runs all the way down to the lake, along the jetty and takes flight. Long limbs dangling, lungs screaming with delight, and nothing can ever be as perfect as that moment before she hits the cold, crisp water below. Carrying her shadow across as far as it will go.

Half a smile creeps onto the lady's face as she watches Pat drag me out of the bus. I feel heavy in my chest like that poor lady does. That's what grief is, knowledge and pain all squashed up together. As me and Pat walk back to the car the grannies open their windows and shout at Pat: 'We know all about your Mabo!' and I asked Pat what his Mabo is but he doesn't say anything. It wasn't my fault getting swept away with everyone. That is a real life defence in court. 'She just got caught up with the wrong crowd, your honour.' Pat didn't have *just cause* to get angry. But he's not one for following the rules.

'Geezus. For the love of…you can't just…take off!'

'Yeah, I can. I'm a bird.'

'You're not a bird, you're a bloody idiot.'

I look outside and see a peregrine falcon hovering in the sky, like she's posing for a still-life painting. I know it's a she because they are bigger then the males. They mate for life and both look after their eggs, which take thirty-three days to hatch. They are the fastest animals in the world except for when they're floating in the sky above you. She's not like the purple-faced eagle that William Freeman drew for my dad. But I wonder if birds can talk to each other, even if one is real and the other is only a picture, drawn a long time ago on a page that's crinkled and torn. Is that falcon up above telling the purple-faced eagle where we are really going?

Pat said he'd lost time, that we were on a schedule and I can't just do what I like. Then the phone rang and his boss Warren got angry with him because he'd sent an order through for some beer, but Pat didn't know what he was talking about. Then he realises I've been pressing buttons on all his technologies.

'You can't keep your bloody hands to yourself, can ya!'

'If God calls, then you should pick up the phone!'

'Stop with all the bullshit! If you'd just be normal none of this would have happened! None of it!'

Subtext is like a truth submarine lying underneath the surface of what people say. Pat knows I understand. It's my fault we've lost Mum. Trouble ends up sticking to me like superglue any which way the wind blows, but am I smart enough to run when the tidal wave reaches shore? Or would I close my eyes and listen to the ocean as it sang me all the way into its dark belly?

9

Why you always park in the middle

What am I afraid of? There's no x + y equation to figure that question out so I get a different answer every time. Pat hasn't said a word for ages. My eyelids close up shop for a while. When I wake up the sun is looking for the other side of the world, taking its bright glare with it. A herd of cattle crosses ahead and Pat slows to a stop. The last cow, she's almost to the other side but then she stops and looks straight at me. Cows never look afraid. They don't care who you are or what you look like. They'll always just stare at you the same and that's why I like them. *Vegetarian egalitarians.*

And now we've made it to Newridge, a town of 147 people that you can actually find on an outback map (of nowhere places no one really cares about). The road in is the road out, a couple of handspans down the track. We pull into car space number three out the front of Midge's Creek Hotel. Halfway between one and five, this third business always leads to trouble, especially when there are ten spaces, but Pat doesn't understand. Pat only sees what numbers look like, not what they *mean*. Mum used to say I could make something feel better if I changed its value. I tried to change the value of huntsman spiders from terrifying to just God-awful until one crawled onto my arm once and I flung it across the room, screaming my head off. Then Mum had to throw magazines at it because that spider kept rearing its front legs up like a shocked horse. The *New Idea* finally got him but he was squashed all over Olivia Newton-John's face and she did not look 'sublime' like the magazine cover said. Just sick.

Spiders are always scary and parking in the third car space is always wrong. You know what Pat says? That someone did a survey in Paris recently and found out that people's favourite number was three. He was trying to trick me into changing its value, but I knew only bad things would happen. Pat looks at a scribbled note on the palm of his hand: '12/3/96, 10.07 am–11.46 am No. 2.' His eyes are five steps ahead. Inside the hotel Pat sees me jiggling and tells me not to cause any trouble, but it's uncomfortable having two needs at opposite ends of your body. I decide to relieve my overextended bladder before I get a lemonade. When I come back from the loo the lemonade's waiting for me with a pink umbrella and a plastic monkey hanging from the side.

I hop onto the bar stool and listen to the horserace on TV. There's a few men watching in the corner, one with a brown cap pulled so far down I can't tell if he's asleep or not.

'Yeah, that O-ring was a bit loose, mate. Anything else?'

Pat's fixing a tap at the bar. Bob the publican shakes his head and looks back at the horses. His mouth's a very thin slit like God had run out of pencil and had to scratch a skinny line with his fingernail so Bob could at least breathe.

Pat glances at the writing on his hand again then acts all casual. 'Got some time up my sleeve then.' He heads towards pokie machine two because he thinks there's still magic inside like there was last time. You can't tell Pat he's put more coins in than he ever gets out 'cause he'll get all huffy and say you don't understand the logic involved in playing.

'How about a washing machine? You got a fridge up your sleeve too?' I'm all sarcastic and Pat glares at me but he knows what I'm talking about. Money owing? Then you got a knockin' coming your way. Every now and then the repo men took a whitegood from Pat's house. Repo men wear singlets stained dark with sweat right through the middle of their chest, who always told Pat they didn't make the rules, they just enforced them.

Days when Pat was real quiet and went out the back of our place to fix something we knew another white-good had been taken. Funny thing is, Pat never really got around to mending anything. Holding the kitchen curtains back I'd watch him just flicking pieces of paint off the verandah staring into space. Once I thought if I made a pretty picture collage out of all that dried paint it would make him forget about the pokies. But the wind always blew those flecks away before I could catch them. So I can't help Pat now like I could never help him back in Beyen. Oprah says we all gotta be agents of change for ourselves so I just sigh like a sad orangutan and watch the horserace on TV.

'*Handsome Prince* has a clear lead, with *Daddy's Little Girl* closing in...'

And that is when it happens. The race caller's voice suddenly becomes like static, all fuzzy and out of focus, then I can't hear him anymore. As they come round the last bend the horses move in slow motion and I hear Mum call the race in French, just like she used to with the potatoes we rolled down the front driveway. She was messaging herself to me through the TV: 'And *3 Times Lucky* comes round the bend, will he make it?' But horse number three came in almost last. This made Mum really upset.

'Oh no, this is a tragedy! As a Frenchwoman I renounce the number three as lucky!'

I was right about the number three and Mum's spirit was trying to protect me. No one else knew what was happening. The punters are either cursing the TV or rubbing their good luck between the palms of their hands. And Pat? Well no surprise there. Flashing colours dance around his face with every coin he slots into his machine. I turn back to the TV but the real race caller's voice is back.

'*Chinese Lantern* coming in there third, with *Lazy Weekender* fourth...'

Why didn't Pat ever believe me? I KNOW about number three and all the corresponding dangers. It goes back to the ancient Greeks and their mythological multiples of three like Cerberus the three-headed dog or Scylla, a sea monster with six heads. Now I have proof from Mum's spirit so I march on over to Pat and clear my throat.

'I don't think the car is all right. I don't think we're okay. I better just check it.'

'Sit and drink your juice.'

'It's not juice, it's lemonade.'

Pat can't take his eyes away from the machine, and because there's always a gap between justice and the law I take the car keys without asking.

Head back towards the toilets then duck out the front. I unlock the car and slide in like liquid. Turn the key, but nothing happens. Then I remember to push down on the pedal at the same time. I slot the car into reverse and shoot across to the other side of the road, put my foot on the brake just before the car rams into the St Vinnie's display window and a rack of half-price winter cardigans. I push the other pedal very gently a few times, slowly forward when another car drives right into the spot I want without asking! So I rear-end it accidentally on purpose.

That is called shit hitting the fan. Pat runs out screaming at me but I can't hear 'cause this big white pillow has exploded in my face and the horn won't stop beeping. Pat told me to always lock the doors if you felt like you were in danger and so that's what I do, but now he was telling me to open up. I push some buttons that just make lights flash and the windscreen-wipers go back and forth and then the sunroof starts to open and Pat jumps up on top of the car like he is a lion in a safari park and falls inside head first. Quick sticks he presses more buttons and the balloon falls away from my face. The noise stops. Then all the people standing on the footpath stare at me and Pat like we're in *Back to the Future* when Marty crashes into that barn and the farm boy thinks he's the spaceman from his comic book. That was funny, but this is not.

This, I thought, is exactly what happens when you do not park in the right spot in the first place. Pat said he was about to win some money because the time and day were all in alignment like the moon in front of the sun. But those machines are never soft on the inside like Turkish Delight; they only make things harder for everyone.

The exploding man says, 'What the bloody hell was she doing?' like I'm not even there. Pat gets out of the car and talks to him in a mumbling voice that adults do when they are trying to put a lid on things. I reach into the back seat and pull out one of the merchandise caps as a sign of goodwill.

'What the fuck is this? I don't want a fucking cap! I don't even drink Coopers!'

Pat grinds his teeth so loud it feels like an earthquake in my ears. He shoves a hand deep down into his pocket and pulls out a lot of money which he gives to the exploding man. Maybe so he could buy a hat of his own choice. All the while Bob is standing in the doorway to the pub and you can't even tell if he's happy or sad because that thin scratchy mouth never moves, not ever. He just shakes his head and goes inside again. And then all the other stodgy sad sacks, as Pat would call them, shuffle after Bob like he's mother duck heading back to the pond. That is the end of the story about why you always park in the middle. Pat was in a Richter-scale-27 mood so I couldn't even tell him about how Mum had talked to me through the TV. *Mon Dieu*!

10

A darkly shadow

The speed dial keeps going up and up. If there was a copper waiting behind a bush he would've clocked us at 143 km per hour. A siren-worthy number. The copper would say, 'A tad too fast for these parts don't you think?' Pat would scrunch the ticket up, drive off and say, 'I play by my own rules.' There was no copper so that didn't happen. This was the real conversation:

'You're a first-class shit, you know that! Do you want me to lose my job?'

'No, that's okay. You can keep it.'

'That was a lot of money, *my* money and I can't get it back! Do you understand that?'

I understood he'd made his own mess, like a dog that pees in his kennel.

'What are the odds? Go on, you tell me what the odds are of you keeping your mouth shut for the rest of the trip.'

I thought this over seriously.

'They are two and six.'

Pat screeches over to the side of the road and stops. He is panting real hard so I think I'll tell him a story. That's what Mum used to do when the buzzing round my head got too loud. I was gonna tell him about my Great Uncle Frederick, who used to eat soap and cigarette butts when he went sleepwalking in the middle of the night, but Pat is having none of it. He bosses me about, says I should get out of the car and find my own way.

'No wonder your mum had a nervous breakdown. You're a bloody handful!'

She didn't get nervous. She got real tired, that one time when I thought my body was turning into metal and I couldn't sleep in case I woke up as a robot with eyes that wouldn't blink.

Nevertheless, I *do* get out of the car and stand by the side of the road while Pat drives off over the hill. The car's all wobbly in the heat waves before it disappears completely. He was blowing off steam. I could wait. But when I'd counted all 183 of the ants making a migraine of a pattern on the ground, Pat was still gone. Some kangaroos lazing about on the open dry grass were looking at me.

Halfway through a bushwalk with Mum I'd once found the foot bone of a roo. It looked wrong all by itself, so long and narrow. When I stare back at those kangaroos, thoughts come into my head. That I am wrong too, standing here like this. Maybe the roos are feeling territorial. Maybe they will come over and kick me out. No trees to hide behind, creek beds to jump down, back doors to run through and home safe. None of that in the here of the now. Land and sky stretching so wide I think the world will never end.

'I am a real girl, not invisible, not a machine, alien or robot. I am a real girl.' I step back and forth so I can see my shadow moving.

'I am a real girl, not invisible, not a machine, alien or robot. I am a real girl.'

In the distance a tiny figure appears. Trouble. Men don't need backpacks unless they are up to no good. In the news police are always taking backpacks from houses they have searched for incriminating evidence.

When I squint real hard that's when I can see. He's black. Blacker than my dad and I can feel his darkness suck the air out of my lungs. Of all the places and times to be alone with no one around except territorial kangaroos. There used to be a safe house in Beyen where you could go if a weirdo was following you home from school. Not here. My own darkness lets him know I am alone and now he will make the earth swallow me whole. He's coming to tear me apart with his angry hands. Turn me deaf with his cyclonic wailing.

Make me blind with his piercing eyes. So I run. I run like a rabbit running from a fox with nothing but fear in my eyes and the boom of my thumping heart. Tina Arena says you can't rely on anyone else for happiness. But also, you cannot rely on anyone else to save you when a black man with a deadly backpack appears in the middle of nowhere.

Unhelpful thoughts and questions tumble out of my head so I can travel faster. Things like a dream I'd once had where this guy got a potplant stuck to the back of his skull and the roots were strangling his brain. And why banana Paddle-Pops taste better than real bananas. But then something extraordinary happens. The kangaroos are running with me. Bouncing high and fast, bodies leaning forward every time their long feet kick off the ground, faster, further, faster, further. They can smell my fear and are trying to show they understand. Feels like I'm competing in an iron-man competition without the swimming and riding. I'm going for gold, going to get away, I'm unstoppable. Until I trip over an old tree root and land with a face full of dirt. Have I lost a tooth? There's something crumbly in my mouth. I spit into the dirt and a large pebble comes out. Get to my feet and quickly assess the damage by triaging myself. There are grazes on my knees and my chin is sore but I can't see if it's bruised. But praise be to God, no blood. No tsunami wave of red coming out of my skin gushing through the dry earth. Mum used to say my fear reached biblical proportions, which made me angry because she only believed in God when she wanted to. Still, I could do with some divine intervention 'cause the man is running towards me and I've lost all my energy. Peed my pants again too. The wet makes a little well in the ground as the man stands over the top of me. He is trying to see into my soul but I won't let him even when he says, 'for the dirt' and I see he's holding out a water bottle for me to wash my eyes. How can I know if his water is pure or has the kind of magic I need? So I don't take it, just get up and keep running. And the look on his face is tattooed on my mind: confused and wounded somehow. For a moment it even looks like the blackness has left him or he's forgotten it was there to begin with and is just a normal man.

He doesn't open his mouth but I know he's saying: 'Where are you going?'

I just want to get out with all five senses and essential organs intact. I think of *Phar Lap* and seeing that big old dead heart of his at the museum. I imagine it pumping in the glass box, big and full of life. I sprint away, with Mum calling the horserace of my life: 'Oh, yes, and *She's a Goer* is on the home stretch now, with *Darkly Shadow* trailing far behind. This filly is a stayer, all the way...'

Then I remember my metal fish. If it rescued me from Dad then surely it would do the same with this fella. I rip it out from the bottom of my bag and hold it in the palm of my hand. Up towards the sky like it's gonna lift me right up and outta here. But my feet don't leave the ground. I do feel vibrations buzzing through my shoes though, travelling up the length of my body all the way to my fingertips. Pat is coming back. Up the road I could see the car wobbling through the heat waves again. He does a U-turn and pulls up beside me, wants to reconcile the situation.

'Righto, now we've had some time to cool down, so let's just zip it for a while whaddyareckon?'

I'm panting so hard I can't answer. He's just staring boggle eyed at the dust and little rivers of wee on my legs.

'What happened to you? Jesus!'

'No, he never showed up. Not even once.'

I yank the handle so hard I think the whole door will fall off. Jump inside and slam it shut. Bam.

'Black travels faster than light, so GO!' I look behind and clock the stranger. I'm not sure if he's looking at me or something further up the road. Standing still makes him look small. And the further we travel, the smaller he becomes until I can't tell him apart from the ground he's standing on. Had I seen a nightmare that wasn't real? I slink down in my seat. Now there is no body of evidence to prove my life had been in danger, Pat would just think I was playing games.

'Look away.' I slide off my peed undies and rummage around in the back for my denim shorts.

'Dylan...'

I know he's trying to find a way back into us.

'Listen, we've just had a blue. No need to—'

'Have a green too?'

Pat goes to say something but then just nods his head.

'Yeah. Spot on.'

I still have my realness because I got the answer right! And I know the truth submarine under Pat's answer was 'You're a weird kid, but you're safe.'

You know they say the Aussie sun is harsh on your skin but the land out here is hard on your mind. It is strange and intangible even though it burrows deep inside of you. The land lives without needing anything but itself. And maybe in this moment I don't need anything except Pat. I push the seat lever and it goes flying back so quick I'm suddenly looking through the sunroof at the bright blue sky.

11

Drawings on the back

Happiness is an energy source. So if you burn it up, hunger is just around the corner. When we pull into the Highett Grove petrol station I'm starving. No chicken tandoori so I have beef and mushroom. I open the pie lid and pour tomato sauce in like engine oil. Pat even got us a mid-sized bottle of Coke each, like we were contemporaries or something. I burp all the way to Pintoori. Did the alphabet twice. Pintoori's a large-scale small town so there's a hotel above the pub even though the only regulars are the bedbugs. One time Pat showed me the bites on his back like he had chicken pox. I choose the left bed and slowly sink into the middle. Pat will have to winch me out in the morning. The air is sticky, makes you feel lazy like golden syrup dripping off a spoon.

Pat puts a big map up on the wall and stands back to take it all in. It's a map of roads, towns, pubs and state lines we'd travel through and across before we got to the ocean, but it's more than that. There is another line through some of those pubs drawn with pink high-lighter, some circled in red. This is a treasure map. I raise a leg into the air and let the breeze from the ceiling fan cool my toes. Pat's nodding his head slowly and crossing something off in his notebook. And just when I think he's forgotten I'm there he says, 'Those teeth aren't gunna brush themselves.'

Fifty brushes upstairs, fifty brushes downstairs, and my teeth are as clean as a century. The tap's leaking and no matter how hard you turn it a slow trickle of water runs down the side of the sink. What a waste of magic. Water has a strength you only see through time. Runs so smooth after hundreds of years its worn great big rocks down to tiny little stones. It doesn't start like a car engine or switch off like a light bulb. Back home it would come through the bathroom taps: water travelling down on the back of a melody. Sometimes it sounded like a whale calling across the sea to its baby, sometimes like a harp with strings made out of early morning spiderwebs covered in sparkly dew. If I hold out my hand, sometimes the song drops will come sit in my palm or balance on a fingertip just like a butterfly.

Water used to protect me from Dad too. If I couldn't get to the hole in the trunk of Barry in time or find the metal fish, I'd imagine myself diving down into the sea where I couldn't hear them fight. The water can be dark and ruthless, don't ever forget that. It can slam you about, steal the life from your lungs before you've got time to come up for air. Wrap you up in a wave and you're gone for good. But in the bathroom it sings. If you play violin or maybe the tuba, you'll be saying, 'Well, are the notes G sharp or E flat?' But I cannot tell you that because the notes I see are colours. The Mongolian monks know. They throat sing about their water which is magic too. For me the low notes are darker in colour. The highest note is clearer than light. But there are no black ones.

I fill two water glasses up, one just shy of the top. If you get the levels right and run a finger round the rim you can sing in harmony. I carry the glasses into the bedroom. Water sloshes up the side but folds back into itself so I don't spill a drop. I place each glass in diagonally opposite corners of the room where the walls meet.

'You don't waste water round here,' says Pat.

It's a scientific fact that genders see things differently and men lack foresight. 'The water is our insurance policy until morning. Night is the loudest time of day and there are many things we cannot know about because they hide in the dark and we ignore them at our peril.'

Pat frowns with confusion. Probably because men also have a limited vocabulary.

'*Peril* is risk and harm combined and water is the antidote.'

'Yeah, yeah, righto. Just go to bed.'

I try, I really do.

Pat turns out the light then sits on the balcony and smokes a cigarette 'cause he thinks that I can't see him. He's breaking a promise to Mum and that makes him feel even worse about it all so he needs another cigarette to calm down. 'It just takes the edge off' is what they say, those people who huddle in a circle out the front of city buildings like a secret tribe trying to make smoke signals. I watch Pat with his feet up on the railing like he's been there for years. Now he's a silhouette of an old man looking down on a sleeping town below, the town he's grown up and old in. Thinking about where the time has gone, the drought of '64 and the flood of '78. The Christmas dance in Mick's shearing shed where he met his wife Meg, buttoned up in the starchy white shirt his mum had ironed special. All the secrets he kept but wishes them long forgotten because he's just too tired to keep holding them anymore.

That's what the quiet time is for, the time between sleeping and dreaming when memories float through the air, twist and turn like vines crawling up to the sun and reach out to rest in someone else's head. The dreams of strangers pass through all the time. They might bring a sadness that's not your own but is bruising all the same.

And your heart can't grow when it's hurting like that. I keep thinking of Mum, where the boat is, who I can be without her. And then I am taken in a dream of my own.

We're right in the middle of a big intersection with cars zooming past and busy businesspeople banging into us. They are cold and unfriendly. Then a man says if I tell him the answer to a riddle I can keep her. But he never tells me what the riddle is. I hold onto Mum's hand until the ground slides away. Then people on buses and in taxis call out to me, talking over one another just to confuse me. And I need all my concentration to hold onto Mum so I scream at them to tell me the riddle and a woman with no eyes turns to me and smiles: 'How long is a piece of string?'

Then she takes Mum's hand and before I can think what the answer might be she slips from my fingers, disappears into the crowd as they shuffle into buildings far away.

I wake up with a start, panting like a dehydrated dog. Even though I hadn't cried in my dream I lick salty tears from the corners of my mouth. Pat is standing over me; says to go back to sleep but I don't want to close my eyes in case I go into the same dream without knowing the answer. I lie on my stomach and ask Pat to draw on my back.

Mum would draw mythical animals like a Centaur, Griffin or a Sphinx. Sometimes even a Teumessian fox, which is so huge that no one can ever catch it. But Pat doesn't know these animals. Mum says Australians have no sense of themselves let alone the history of the world and even though Pat said that was a bit harsh he still doesn't know that man-eating birds with beaks of bronze and sharp metallic feathers are called Stymphalians.

Pat says we have a big day ahead of us tomorrow and that we both need to get some sleep. He wipes my face with one of his hankies and it smells a little bit like the eucalyptus lollies he keeps in his pocket so Mum doesn't know he's been smoking. He says I should just try to think of something nice, but I say that everything nice has a picture of Mum in it somewhere. I ask Pat why, apart from when Mum died, had I never seen him cry, not even once. Pat sits on my bed and for the longest time he says nothing. Then he says that once the floodgates are open it's hard to close them again. The shadow of Pat's hand reaches towards me. I think he's going to draw like I want him to and I don't even care if it was something unmythical like a stapler or a pineapple. But he got startled by his own silhouette. Got up and lay down on the other bed. He still had that old man's sadness as well as his own.

I watched Pat that night, watched as his breathing got slower and slower and heavy with stories travelling through the night air. We would have to take turns looking out for one another. Even though Pat was older than me, he still needed someone to stay near when he was scared and thought that dam would burst. Suddenly I had the answer to that riddle—I knew how long a piece of string was. Twice as long as half of it.

12

Lending time

Some things you just can't return to, least not straight away. And when you wake from a dream, it's like missing the bus. Another will come around the corner but it might take you somewhere else. Even though I stepped back into sleep, I couldn't find the building where those people had taken Mum. Couldn't find that cold grey place at all. So in the morning I wrote down the riddle and the answer just in case that bus came back another night. Pat was shaving in the bathroom and I had to pee real bad so I lay back on the bed and stretched my legs up and over my head so it wouldn't trickle out.

'How will Mum know where the boat is if she doesn't have the same map as us?'

Pat's razor stops halfway down his cheek. 'Mothers know everything.'

Pause button off, the razor slides down to his chin.

It was true but not the answer I'd asked for. I stretch

my toes out but get a cramp in the little one. Pain shoots up my foot and I remember that I've still got a balloon for a bladder. Upright myself and dash past Pat, pull my undies down and…there it goes.

'Hey, I ain't—whaddya—'

'It's a human right.'

'Takin' a piss?'

'Knowing where your mother is.'

'You know where she's buried. And you're here with me until we get to—'

'But where is *omnipresent*? If her spirit is everywhere then why isn't she here now when I want to talk to her?'

Pat wipes his face clean with a face cloth. Missed a few spots but that's not what he's looking at. He's staring at me in the mirror with puppy-dog eyes like he's gonna 'fess up to stealing a Mars bar from the corner shop twenty years ago.

'Dylan, I need to show you something…'

Fingers tap his back pocket but then he just rubs the rough patches of stubble on his face. Figures it's not the time or place for secrets, and the only thing he finds is that furrowed brow again.

'The eggs are shithouse downstairs so we're going across the road.' Cleans out his razor, flicks it twice on the sink and walks out. That tap is still running. I turn it an inch to the right but it makes no difference at all. The girl staring back in the mirror looks younger than me. She'll need to catch up if she wants to stay with me. Brushing my hair, I tell her I know some things are best left forgotten until you're ready to stop running. I brush until all the curls are gone and it's just one big ball of fuzz, like when cartoon characters get an electric shock and everyone laughs. But it's not funny. People used to call me Velcro at school; laugh and wink like I was in on the joke too.

I used to brush Mum's hair forever, just because I could. Start at the top and slide through like butter, that brush would. Being white is easy. You don't have to pretend to be anything else. I pull extra hard on knots at the back of my head. It hurts, so I do it again.

'I don't care which direction they run in, you eat those eggs.'

Sitting at the cafe across from the pub I slit them like a qualified surgeon. Lucky I have compliant yolks 'cause I'm not eating anything that travels south and Pat has no jurisdiction to make me. Mum said sometimes living with me and Pat was like being stuck between two mules and she even drew a little cartoon of her getting squished between two big donkey bums with her eyes popping out of her head. Well, I'm fed up with Pat and his bossing me about.

'I've got lots of secrets in here,' I say, rummaging around in my backpack.

'Good on ya, mate.'

'Smart-arse.'

'Watchyamouth.'

'Watch ya nose.'

Even though it wasn't a special occasion and I don't like things around my neck, I put on Mum's air loom necklace. Then I pull out my special fork and wave it back and forth to show Pat I mean business. He's rummaging round in his mind for something to say, but he's left it too late for a comeback. The waitress says Pat's card hasn't gone through. He has to pay in coins like the grey brigade on pension day. A five-cent piece falls off the table and spins round. I bet tails but it goes between the floorboards so I'll never find out if I'm right.

Reckon I was 'cause when we shove our bags in the car there are *still* no clouds in the sky. Pat is mumbling to himself and keeps checking both sides of his wallet like he'd missed some money first time round. You can't just wish money into existence because then everyone would have some and the currency would devaluate. *Detonate. Evaporate.*

Pat doesn't put anything away because he has holes in his pockets; money just slips straight through. I told Mum she should just sew up the inside of his pockets like lady pants from Kmart, but she said that wouldn't help. Now Pat's just staring at me, or Mum's necklace to be precise. His eyes don't blink not even once until I snap my fingers right in his face like he's been hypnotised.

'Wakey wakey.'

He bends down to tie his shoelace even though it's already in a double knot. Sneaks a glance across the road. That's where his eyes find what they're looking for.

The pawnshop is a toy store for grown-ups. In this one I find a fox head with a long tail attached that you wrap around your neck for warmth. I reckon it's from the 1930s when everyone was depressed and had no money to buy a proper coat so they had to use animals instead. Then I put on an eye patch with faded green velvet on the outside and 'ahoy' written in red glitter. I also find a Viking hat that has two horns, one on each side. It was made out of plastic because you can't conquer with a heavy head. There's music playing from somewhere and a guy singing about 'takin' my baby back home again'. If I could find some dance shoes my outfit would be complete. You don't see many jazz-tapping, depressed pirate Vikings. Pat's talking to the guy at the front about his watch.

'It's worth at least five hundred bucks.'

'I'll give you seventy.'

Pat scoffs at the man like it's highway robbery, but nods anyway. I think his dad gave it to him before he got lots of dust in his lungs from building houses and had to carry a tank of air round with him all day. The man was just lending Pat some time; he'd get the watch on the way home again. Or so he said. The man behind the counter nodded at me and said I could keep the Viking helmet. Can you believe it?! Free history! Pat just looked at me, smiled.

'You are one lucky kid.'

Even though it was my fault we'd lost all the money sometimes it felt like we were on the same team. Maybe we'd run out of angry or maybe we were just tired of staring down the same neverending road. By the time Wanteegi rolled around we were silent partners. Like old married couples who know what the other is thinking. Pat would put his hand out just before I reached for the Minties. I'd play a Johnny Farnham song in my head and he'd start singing it. It was like this lady who lived in New York with a parrot. One day she was just thinking to herself about going for a walk and at the very same time her parrot—who was in another room—squawked out 'Better take a jacket!' Or Bobby the tortoise-shell cat who was left behind when his owners moved so he walked across the entire country until one Tuesday the owner opens the door and Bobby jumps onto the couch like he's just been out for bit of fresh air.

'Where do you hear all this stuff?'

'I keep my senses on. You never know when you're gonna be smacked in the head with a good story.'

We haven't seen anything living on land or in the air for miles but right at that moment, two big splats of bird poo land square in the middle of the windscreen. Pat tries to get them off with the wipers but there's no water left in them so the poo smears everywhere and we can't see a thing.

Screech to a halt. The only liquid in the car is a half-empty bottle of Coke so we pour it over the windscreen and wipe it off with tissues. I look at Pat and we start laughing our heads off. Laughing is emotional medicine; some people in China stand in a circle and giggle together. Leaning against the bonnet we're suddenly thinking the same thing again—Mum would have loved this.

When you forget you're grieving, laughter is a guilty treat. Soon enough Pat packs his smile away in its box. Can't tell what, but there's something else he's feeling guilty about too.

Wanteegi, now that's a strange place. So much dust it bleeds out the soles of people's skin leaving red foot-prints all over town. The men are tall and skinny and the women short and fat—like some kind of genetic rule. The kids? They were just plain weird—caught somewhere between the short and tall of their folks. Nothing much grows here on account of the dust, so people only eat veggies from a tin with steak done one of three ways. Rare, rarer and still beating. Worse still,

I reckon all that tin-can metal has been seeping into their brains, tampering with neurons. At the Watering Hole Hotel the barmaid plonks a lemonade down in front of me. Gritty eyes and fidgety lips. Hair last washed a couple of weeks ago.

'We run out of them plastic monkeys.'

Which was okay by me. 'There's too much plastic in the world and it's choking the seals. Sometimes they wash up on the beach wearing the necklace of death,' I say.

'We ain't nowhere near the sea. So don't you worry about that.' She has a rotten tooth up front and her fingertips are stained yellow. Pat comes over and points at the pokies.

'How long they been here?'

'Few weeks.'

'Which one's put out the most?'

'You gonna take number four out for Chinese or somethink?'

She pulls up her bra strap up and starts stacking glasses. Pat smiles at her but not in a nice way. He heads over to Ted the publican whose real name is Edward but no one calls him that except his mother and she is dead too. I check the cardboard-cutout man is in optimal viewing position. Even though he had eyes, he couldn't really *see* so I get a green pencil from my backpack and poke looking holes through—now I'm incognito.

By the look on Ted's face, Pat had stuffed something up again but this time it couldn't be my fault. I hadn't touched his phone since I got on that bus with all the Yankee grannies.

'But I ordered 370 of the lager. You'll have to take it back.'

'That's 40 cents off a unit, off your package rate if—'

'Who's drinking that here? Couldn't give it away.'

Ted does a double take and squints in my direction. Cover blown, abort mission.

Pat storms over and talks real quiet like he's telling me a secret, except he's real mad. That's what adults do when they want to shout but have to show some *restraint.*

'Go outside and pretend you're a statue. One that doesn't move.'

That didn't make any sense, but I stop myself from saying so and finish my lemonade. The barmaid pays no attention. Margie would have called her a floosie shantoosie. But I felt sorry for her. Somehow I knew that inside her lungs something was growing. One day she'd go to the hospital for her hacking cough and never leave.

13

Broken bottles

Out the back of the pub I hear a ratbag boy jeering, and even before I turn the corner I know he's a prime example of Wanteegi's genetic misfits. Squished nose, freckled face, squinty eyes and a front lip curled up on the right like he got nipped by a fishhook. Old-man knobbly knees and untied shoelaces. Ripped T-shirt and ears so full of dirt you could grow potatoes. There are three of them and this Mr Freckle-face is in charge. His brother wears a permanent scowl on account of his forehead that juts out like a cliff edge. The last one is a hanger-onna. They call him Dagbum and he can't be much more than four. He just stares at me and keeps playing with his willy like he needs to go to the toilet.

Freckle-face tells Scowler to put all these glass bottles up on the wooden fence posts so he can shoot them down with a slingshot. He isn't very good. Heaps of stones just zoom past. Then one hits the middle bottle and it explodes. I watch as all the pieces shatter into tiny glass diamonds. For a moment it looks like a crystal ball floating in mid-air and it's beautiful. But a split second later those pieces are falling. The bottle can never be fixed and made useful again and that is the same as not being alive. I run over and count all the pieces of glass. There are sixty-eight, which makes me sad because that is a whole number and it very much wasn't. Then Freckle-face tells me to rack off, that I shouldn't be there. I tell him what I think about this disgraceful waste but he just laughs and says they were meant to be broken so I can piss off now and let him get back to it. I'm scared all right, but my feet sink a little deeper into the dirt. Some things are worth holding your ground for.

Freckle-face starts up with the slingshot again and another bottle explodes right near my head. A shard of glass actually goes into my hair. I found it that night in the shower when it pricked my finger. He aims another one at me but it goes straight past and hits a rabbit that was running away. It's motion *less*. I saw that one other time with a myna bird. He was hopping up and down on a brick wall at school then just fell off. Died in the one moment I'd been watching him. Does the rabbit feel that split second when life and death run into each other?

I crouch next to it, perfectly soft and warm. I'm dizzy and I close my eyes, but then I'm back in the tree and Mum's falling forever.

Which world am I in; is this real? Am I a real girl?

There's a volcano stirring inside and my blackness is rising to the surface, too late to stop it. I run over to the bottles and smash every single one. Slam them into each other until there's a giant puddle of glittering glass, a mirage of sparkling splinters. Nothing pretty about it. Nothing at all.

Before I can do anything else Freckle-face whispers in Scowler's ear. He comes running over and pulls my hair so hard I fall over backwards. Kicks me in the guts and I curl into myself like an echidna. Then everything's dark. But I hear Freckle-face egging him on.

'Harder!'

Scowler doesn't say anything and I think maybe he's thought better of it. But then there's a boot in my back and my spine's burning. Again and again. I peek through my fingers and look up at him. His face is blank but tears are running down his cheeks. The little one comes over and stares at me.

'Dirty.'

He wasn't talking about the muck in my hair or the dust choking me in the throat. But I am not the colour he thinks I am. I am not black. I'm invisible, like water.

Freckle-face comes over and spits in my eyes.

'Piss off, you ugly cunt.'

That word cuts right through me and out the other side. Pierces my chest and lets all the air out. I'm suffocating and want the ground to take me now.

'Fuck off, the lotta-ya!'

Pat marches over arms flapping and feet pounding. Before they know what's what he's yanking them off me and up into the air. Freckle-face falls to the ground, but he's not afraid.

'She broke all the bottles!'

'And what were you doing, then? Fuck off! GAWN!'

They scramble to their feet and around the back of the pub, cut across the laneway opposite and behind a row of houses. As the dust settles Pat looks down and I'm sure he's about to throw me through the air too.

'You gonna crawl into a ball every time ya get in trouble?'

'It was running, just running, that's all.' I point to the dead rabbit on the ground.

'I'm not always gonna be here, right?'

Before I can ask where else he'll be, Pat curls my hands into fists. Puts his own up and jiggles round like a boxer, motions me forward, but I'm too sore to move so I stay put. He takes one of my fists and hits his chest with it. Nods and eggs me on but I'm not playing this game. So he hits me gently on the shoulder. Just mucking around but takes me by surprise and I stumble back.

'People will hurt you if you let them. And you won't understand it, but they'll do it anyway.'

I'm a lover not a fighter, so I don't retaliate. Pat gives up and walks away. (Mum says that's what men do best.) I crouch down next to the rabbit and stroke his fur. He shouldn't be alone, being freshly dead, so I put him in my backpack. Suddenly I'm angry that not one single thing will change. Those boys will be back breaking and killing tomorrow and I can't do anything about it except let my fury off the leash right now. I run up to Pat and whap him on the back. Never saw it coming so he falls to the ground and I'm punching him in the chest: 1, 2, 1, 2. Then we're rolling around in the dirt like animals and it feels good just to think with my hands. When we've got nothing more to give I get to my feet. Pat reaches out and I pull him up.

Taking a grown man down's not something to brag about so when we're back in the car I put a lid on my smile and buckle up. Pat, on the other hand, is beaming from ear to ear as he reverses the car out, arm stretched over the back of my seat.

'You gotta good hook. Could make a career outta that,' says Pat.

'Lady fighters are down-and-out dogs,' I say back.

'Says who?'

So I tell Pat about the lady politician who wanted to ban women in the ring because it wasn't proper letting their female bits get bruised and battered about. It mucked up the cycles of femininity she said.

Pat goes all red in the face and doesn't know where to look. 'Well, yeah, okay. All I know is you got a crackin' uppercut on ya.'

I watch as a skinny-fat family push their little three-legged terrier in a pram down the street.

So long, Weirdsville. Thanks for the punch in the guts.

14

178 little specks

'Where'ya puttin' it all? You're skinny as a rake.'

'I have a fast metamorphosis.'

'Righto.'

That night we got to Gummagi, which has a pub but not one Pat has anything to do with, so he let me get ribs as a special treat. Pat didn't really touch his honey prawns and to be honest I don't blame him. They were covered in pink gunky sauce, and anyways, where did they find prawns out here in the middle of the bush? I reckon they're golden-syrup yabbies but I don't tell Pat in case he kicks up a stink. So it's only when I get napkins for my sticky fingers that I see Pat looking at me. Shifts his prawns round on the plate like dodgem cars banging into one another.

'Your Mum...did she ever say anything about me?'

'Like what?'

'You know...about the future...feelings...'

The waitress comes over with another beer for Pat.

'How is everything?'

I look at Pat's fluorescent prawns. 'Bit bright don't you think?'

She glances at the ceiling, then turns to Pat like he's my translator.

'Lights don't go down 'til seven.'

Some people pretend they can't see me. But invisibility like that doesn't make me feel good. She takes my plate without asking. There was all this sauce I'd saved for the end, but I can't call out because suddenly Pat's choking on one of those yabbies. Eyes bulging he leans across the table just in case it crawls back out on its own. I jump up and whack him on the back like I think you're supposed to. All I can hear is the sound of other people's cutlery clinking on their plates as they stop eating and watch like gagging is a spectator sport. Then I remember it's the Heinrich movement I'm supposed to be doing. I wrap my arms around his middle and yank hard. The prawn pops out and back onto his plate.

Pat downs his beer in one go then clears his throat like a tyre skidding on gravel.

'I think we'll have the bill.'

At 3.27 am I wake up from another nightmare. Cockroaches, hundreds of them trying to eat my eyes out so I can't find the boat. Mum's calling my name but now I'm blind it makes no difference. That purple-eyed eagle flies down and tries to eat the cockroaches but its claws end up scratching my face and I wake myself up before the blood comes pouring out of my eyes.

Part of the dreaming world is still here. I can feel the bugs all over my body and the eagle flapping at the window. I call out to Pat but he's not there so I grab my backpack and run downstairs. In the pub bistro the clocks have stopped hours ago and people are wandering through time fast or slow as they please. Pat's at the pokies in the gaming room. Though his eyes are half shut he offers a dozy smile. I try to tell him there's a plague in the bedroom but he waves me quiet.

'It's systemic—systematic, Dylan. You have to believe in the system!'

He giggles, then looks at me like he's only just realised I'm there. 'They'll sing to you,' he whispers.

The machines don't care who's feeding them. There's a gadget inside that'll play a song no matter who hits the button. Flashing lights glow through my fingertips. I tell him about the dream but he just agrees that cockroaches could be a real bugger and next time maybe I should wear an eye mask when I go to bed so they can't get me. I needed him to say it would be okay and that I could go back to sleep and my eyes would not see the same thing, but he just gave me some money for the jukebox and told me to go cheer myself up.

I knew as soon as I saw the playlist. Johnny Farnham's 'Burn for You'. There's only a few couples on the dance floor and a swaying drunk with his eyes closed, talking to someone who isn't there. I take the snow globe out of my backpack. Shake it up and watch all the tiny snowflakes fall softly around the Eiffel Tower. 178 little specks of white floating through watery air. There's me and Mum climbing up that tower staring at a city where the streetlamps turn into a thousand fallen stars and someone somewhere plays music on a wind-up box, a tinny song everyone half remembers from long ago. I hold the snow globe up to my eyes and look through it. This time I see Mum for real. She's on the dance floor beckoning me over. But I don't go. It's her turn to listen:

'You have to call, otherwise people won't know where you are,' I tell Mum.

I know she'll be gone, but I take the snow globe away from my face anyway.

'You might make them feel bad, don't you know that?' I say to her even though she's not there.

The corners of the room are etched in darkness and suddenly that drunk with his twelve-beer breath is dancing with me. Too much, too close. All the little pock-marks in his face where the whiskers come out and glassy bloodshot eyes drowning in *missed opportunities*. He stumbles round squeezing me closer and closer. When he laughs I can see gold in his mouth and a wicked tongue that wants to tell me things I should not know. I try to get away but he's too strong and I'm too sad for my mama. All the colours of his boozy song run into each other like a dirty puddle. I can feel him get hard in places that men are supposed to keep to themselves. Not for me, not for me, not in this place, not ever.

'I'm a real girl, I'm a real girl,' I say so I'm not stolen away by the fear of it all. And then the only thing I can hear is the sound of my teeth grinding together.

Boom, *boom*, *boom*. My giant is back again. Pat rips that man off me like he's snapping a pistachio shell in two. Crack! He spins round trying to stay on his feet but crashes into other people who knew what was going on but turned away. Someone shouts at Pat like *he's* done the wrong thing!

I don't want to be there with strangers' eyes pecking at my face like hungry birds. Pat takes my hand and we stumble back up to the bedroom. He asks if the man had touched my private parts and I say everywhere is private when I don't want to be touched.

He puts me into bed and now I can't even remember why I was downstairs in the first place. I want to start again, go back and be a tiny baby who doesn't know anything yet. I want nothing in my mind except white space.

'I didn't get to her in time,' is all I can say.

Pat sits down and draws on my back, keeps me in the room away from the loud, the hurt, the echoes of all that we've lost.

'Ssshhh. You're gonna be safe there. For real, for real,' Pat slurs. 'Where?' I want to ask. When we get to the boat? Or Paris, back in the belonging? My mouth is drowsy and I have to close my eyes. He's drawing the outline of a heart over and over, making a tattoo on my skin. I'm back on the Eiffel Tower again watching 178 little specks of snow float slowly past.

15

Rabbit pie

Dreams chase me down again as soon as my head hits the pillow and I'm far away from that tower in the snow globe, trying to climb a mountain with Pat. We hear a low rumble. He says it's only thunder but I know it's coming from the sea, building up and taking everything in its path. All the starfish, seaweed, crabs and sharks. Pat keeps saying all we need is tissues but I don't know what that means. The rumbling gets louder until I wake up. There's light streaming out from underneath the toilet door. I'm afraid but creep over all the same.

'Pat?'

'Why did ya do that? Take her away from me?'

I peek through the narrow slit between the door and the wall and inside Pat sits on the toilet, head in his hands.

'We had something goin', ya know?'

He opens the door and shoves a little box into my face. Inside is a ring. Maybe he was gonna go on one knee in the middle of a pricey seafood restaurant where everyone would put their lobsters down to clap.

'We were gonna *be* something! And now it's all gone. Why did ya take her away from me?'

I had stones in my belly weighing me down because it was true. I should have stayed inside Margie's house and eaten my Monte Carlo biscuits. Then everything would have been okay. Pat wasn't playing *The Price is Right*. This was *Tonight Is All Wrong*. You can't just plug holes with another person's glue. I heard that on *The Phil Donahue Show*, about a man called Ferone who had five wives in three different states 'cause each one of them was a little bit like his high-school sweetheart who'd run off with a Texan rodeo clown called Cordell. And now I see all of that plugging we'd done for each other hadn't worked because Pat's dam had burst and the only thing I had for him was a home-brand tissue, crumpled up but still new. I straighten it out and slide it underneath the door. It doesn't feel as soft as it should.

After a moment he comes out, puts his jacket on and heads back downstairs, pretending like he never cried in the first place. But if you don't cry you can drown from the inside out.

I go back to bed but this time there are no dreams

following me.

Early morning light flickers. Out the window in the tall ghost gum newborn maggies are gabbling with hunger. It doesn't look like a nice way to eat, having a worm rammed down your throat. But nature's not always pretty. I heard some guy on TV say that when he'd just seen a monkey eat another monkey's baby.

Who knows what time Pat came back last night. I poke him but he just rolls over like a walrus sleeping on the beach. They are best left undisturbed. But then the phone rings. He falls out of bed and stumbles across to the dresser.

'Yeah, nah, I'm on my way. Be there round lunch. Yeah well…been a few hiccups along the way.'

He looks straight at me.

'I understand that, Brian.' Which is code for *I'd like to bung you over the head, Brian.*

'Na. We're good.'

And he looks at me again.

This time, I nod.

It isn't long before a small rattle underneath the car bonnet turns into a chug chug chink and then a non-stop grind. I have a pair of stockings in my bag for special occasions—or a fanbelt—but Pat says this is a problem that needs a bank loan to fix. So my brain's thinking ahead to a worst-case scenario: we break down and Pat's got no phone coverage. A goods truck finds the car weeks later, but we're long gone. A search and rescue party is sent out. Finally helicopters spy us crawling through the desert. We're out of Coke and I'm not drinking my own pee so they've come just in time. We're winched up to safety and it's high fives all round. The papers print a photo of me wrapped in a foil rescue blanket.

But for now that's all just a hypothetical scenario. After 457 thumps and bangs we make it to Boorilliak and pull up out front of the Shearer's Arms. (Why don't pubs talk about people's legs?) This pub smells like the boys' toilet at school where the preps accidentally piss on the floor because they can't aim straight. Pat's on the phone again. 'Yeah, I know it's overdue, I put a cheque in the post yesterday.'

That's not true 'cause we haven't seen a postbox for ages. I guessed Pat had lost another whitegood. Maybe his washing machine. Mum said one day he wouldn't own anything except his fillings. Can you imagine, the fridge, washer, TV and even the three-piece settee. There isn't a slot big enough but somehow the pokies have swallowed the lot and made a liar out of Pat.

He puts on a business smile as the publican nods him over to the bar. This is Brett who must have tapeworms in his gut because really, all I can see is skin and bone. There are tiny ones sticking out the side his nose and ears and he looks like a cartoon stick figure. Meanwhile his wife who makes the counter meals—today there's pork chops and peans (peas and beans)—has a stringy mop of grey hair and I kept thinking Mum could have done a really nice perm, made her face a bit softer.

'Had a lady come in the other day, sat right where you are,' she says like we're picking up from where we left off last week. Her boobs jiggle up and down as she shoves the tea towel round the inside of a glass. 'Was talking to who I imagine was her daughter—something similar in the eyes, you know?'

I nod because sometimes people just want a sounding-board.

'She was telling the daughter that her own folks used to run this pub back in the 40s, way before me and Brett ever thought we'd end up this way. Said she remembered how the bathroom was right above the front bar and one time her three sisters had been muckin' about with the taps and flooded the bathroom. Water dripped through the ceiling and onto some poor punter's head sitting right here having a port, would you believe, at four o'clock on a Wednesday afternoon.'

I look up at the ceiling and there are still wriggly brown water stains on the roof. That was one long bath.

'You wouldn't believe it but the bloke sitting next to this lady turns to her and says, "Yeah, and you still owe me a refill." If it wasn't our Tommy who's sitting on the same bar stool a good fifty-something years later! With his port! I mean what are the chances?'

I thought about it for a while. I mean I really thought about it because this was a complicated one. 'They are 22 and 30.'

She's not bothered by my answer. She laughs with one big hoot. 'If they didn't go and buy him a two-litre bottle of port from behind the bar here! Can you imagine, all for our Tommy! Ah, dear, that was a day.'

An oven timer rings and she brings out a shepherd's pie for Barney who's a Vietnam Vet and thinks ASIO is microwaving his house. Just to be sure, he keeps his chickens in an underground coop. He pays for pub meals in eggs and lemons from the tree in his backyard. Now, I know all this but I don't *know* Barney. Nevertheless he turns to me before leaving and says: 'The tides don't wait.'

Barney's mouth was moving, but it was Mum who spoke.

'Pay no mind and mind me language, but Barney's still pissing out Agent Orange,' says Brett's wife, flicking pastry flakes off the counter.

Pat's still busy with Brett so I'm hoping that Barney might let Mum talk to me a little more. But he's already doing a U-turn in his battered old Kingswood by the time I make it outside. On the bottom step of the entrance hall a little girl's playing with a slinky, scratching her head like a monkey with lice.

She takes three jellybeans out of her pocket—two green and one black—and places them in the middle of her palm. Squints at me for a second then nods, so I sit on the step beside her. She slowly holds her hand out and I take a green one.

'I don't like the black ones either,' she says.

We sit and suck on our jellybeans until they turn into clear blobs all slippery and flat. I am eyeing off her slinky because it is all the colours of the rainbow. She puts it on the top step and we watch it slink down over itself again and again. Every step a different colour.

'Do you want to swap it for my rabbit?' I think that is a reasonable transaction and her eyes open wide with excitement. So I take out the poor little bunny I'd been keeping in my backpack. Hold him by the scruff of the neck like mama animals do and he sways gently in the wind.

The girl pokes him with her finger and screams.

'Ssshhh, he's sleeping,' I whisper.

Some people are scared of dead things and I understand the girl wants something in-between, either alive or a toy, but I didn't have either. She runs back inside and gets Brett's wife who is apparently also her granny.

I think she's gonna blow her top but she just cocks her head to the side: 'Well…it's been a while between rabbit pies.'

16

Flutter by

My rabbit didn't make it into a pie and I did not get the slinky.

Pat comes out to see what all the hoo-ha is about. He reels back when I open my backpack and I don't blame him. Death smells if you don't burn it or bury it. Pat says I can't carry the rabbit round with me even if it had been an injustice. 'Only thing you can do is write a letter to the department of…animal cruelty,' he says. While we drive out of town Pat tells me to look out for a good place to bury it. I see a few along the way but I'm not ready to let go yet so don't say anything. Doesn't matter 'cause in the end that rabbit chooses his final resting place.

I tell Pat to pull over, and I get out and climb under a barbed-wire fence. Pat looks a little bit worried about it all but I just keep on walking 'cause this rabbit knows where it wants to go. Snap and crack stepping over old, bendy twigs. Bark peeling off ghost gums like wall-paper pulled halfway down. And then we stop. This is the place right in the middle of a circle of trees, happy to watch over him for all time. Pat gets on digging a hole. There is always a 'sleeping shovel' in the back of his ute in case he hits a roo and has to put it out of its misery. I stroke the rabbit a few more times. Leave lines in his fur with my fingers so he'll know someone was with him. The wind changes direction and flickers along the dry grass up the hill, tells everyone to settle down and stay still. I lie the rabbit down and watch as Pat covers his body with dirt. Hovering above I'm like a clumsy ogre with long limbs.

Some people say that nothing is the opposite of everything, but I don't think so. Nothing can be silence and light and that is worth a lot in a world full of angry noise. Space is nothing and everything at the same time. It's where we came from and where we return. Soon big clumps of dirt cover the rabbit's head and he's gone, wrapped up in the earth.

'Can he keep Mum company?'

'I don't know about that.'

'Maybe they'll be looking for potatoes.'

'Do rabbits eat potatoes?'

'They eat whatever the good Lord provides.'

I don't know if that is true. My rabbit could've been a fussy eater like Atticus Barnes who only ate devon and tomato-sauce sandwiches on white bread. Pat rummaged in his pocket and took out a clothes peg. It was yellow and faded, the plastic cracked in the middle. Sometimes Pat would do his washing at our house—when the repo man took his last washer away he did it all the time. When he hung out a load he'd always have pegs sticking out of his mouth. Sometimes when I was in his good books Pat would take the last peg and chase me round the garden, snapping it like a crazy duck. I always told him to stop even though I didn't mean it. He looks at me now and snaps the peg. We run and run like that paddock is the back garden stretching on forever and teatime is a long way off.

Pat pretends he has a lame leg so I can beat him but then he speeds up and runs past me.

'Oldest trick in the book, ya daft chook!'

I think I'll show him so I run off in the other direction. Back through the gum trees and the tall grass swooshing this way and that. I can feel her warm hand on my back and I know that when I get to the other side of the trees I'll find water. So sure that Mum will look after me. I close my eyes. Just walk through the bush until the dam is right in front of me. Having water is a human right so no one can stop me from swimming in it.

'Dylan, Dylan!'

I strip down to my crop top and undies. Wading in

I feel mud slide between my toes. It's slippery and cold. After being cooped up in a car for the past few days this feels like heaven.

'DYLAN!!!!' Pat's still a long way off. He's screaming now.

I paddle out and duck under. The water's happy to see me too, humming deep like a purple and burnt-orange note together—what a beautiful harmony those two make. I swim under all the way to the other side. When I come up a crow's wings flap overhead heavy in flight. She's gliding away from the sun, scared the heat will melt her beak clean off.

Wing shadows pass over Pat who's standing on the edge of the dam. 'What the bloody hell are you doing? You just pissed off! Again!!!!'

'I could hear the water.'

'You can't hear a dam.'

'Yes you can. If you listen loudly.'

'Get out!'

'Get in!'

'GET OUT!'

'GET IN!!!'

Pat is none too pleased with me.

'I'm not having this, Dylan. Stop piss-farting around and get out.'

'We need the water. It's a life force. Plus, you stink.'

•

This was true on all accounts. The shower hadn't worked at the last pub and when it jolted into action all that came out was brown stuff with sandy bits in it.

Pat takes his boots off at the edge of the dam and all the hot botheredness comes out like steam from an oven. He paces up and down in the shallow bit like he is still thinking of something to say. Water molecules vibrate faster than the speed of sound and slow everything down. I reckon that's why Mum had led me here in the first place, so I could help Pat slow his flustered heart. He takes his shirt off, splashes some water on his face and under his armpits.

'All right, you've had ya fun, now move.'

But I just hold out my hand. You have to be patient with people who are scared.

Slowly, he comes in deeper until the water's up to his nipples. Pat can't swim but I just keep holding out my hand. I look at him like Crocodile Dundee staring down that big old water buffalo. Hard to believe a man like Pat could be scared of something so beautiful. That he can't see how it will help his body heal itself.

But then he lets go. Enough for me to guide him into the middle of the dam where the mud disappears below and you have to float. He takes a sharp breath in.

'I can't...'

He struggles at first, tries to turn back and get out, but I'm under him before he knows what's happening. I push his legs to the surface until he is floating and can't do anything but stare straight up…and then he lets the water take his weight. I do the same and I'm back home. Mum's defrosting the fridge, eating pieces of ice as she goes. Pat's got his legs up on the table, pushing the chair back like a cocky schoolboy showing off. There'll be chicken and chips for dinner and I've got a Golden Gaytime as a special arvo treat.

I look over and Pat's floating on the water by himself. He's waiting to walk through the back door of a memory as well.

The first time I met Pat, Mum kept staring at me like I was a lab rat and no one's sure if the experiment's gonna work out. She sipped her shandy all quiet and polite and Pat kept looking round the bar like he had someone else to meet. I counted Pat's fillings up the back of his mouth, which I could see when he threw peanuts down his throat. Two on one side, three on the other. Dirty gold colour. After a while they forgot I was there. Mum smiled when Pat whispered something in her ear even though she pretended to be shocked. Some people say they don't like games and just want to get real, but adults play all the time. Mum said Pat was a bit rough around the edges and that is what she liked about him most. Back home in France, people wouldn't know what to do if a snake crawled into their living room and curled up asleep under the TV. But Pat did. Got a long stick with pincers on the end, grabbed it by the neck and shoved it in a brown sack. Twisted it round so the snake got dizzy then drove it halfway out of town. Back home in France the men would wail like a baby if they were fixing a fence and some barbed wire pierced their hand so deep it looked like it would come out the other side. But Pat just snipped the wire off on the other end, drove himself to hospital and said, 'Think I might need some snitches.' Of course he meant stitches but by then he'd lost a litre of blood and was about to collapse. And even though Pat could not dance like a Parisian, he had his own little moves that made Mum giggle and that is better than knowing the right steps. Like when he wiggles the first finger on each hand pretending to be an AFL umpire. Or sticks his hip out to the side like he's shutting a car door. Mum would laugh and laugh. And I liked it when Pat danced with me too. He'd spin me round until everything turned into a blurry rainbow and I was proper dizzy. He'd always catch me before I fell. But sometimes Pat came over to the house, thoughts swirling round his head. He'd just sit on the couch with his mouth closed tight. One night we brushed the flies off a lamb roast for an hour and a half because he was so late. When he did finally come Mum only talked to me.

'Dylan, why do you call when you're going to be late?' she said.

'Because you might make someone worry.'

I was happy 'cause I'd got the answer right, but Pat just took out a beer from the fridge, cracked it open and finished it in one gulp. Then he said, 'Now listen…' and that's when you're supposed to leave the room. However I was starving so I shoved a forkful of peas in my mouth. I knew it was stupid but Mum was still trying to talk to Pat *through* me and it all became a bit of a mess. If only I'd forked up a piece of roast potato first. White food before green. Always. I stuck a finger down my throat to start again but Mum yanked it out. She said if I ate in reverse everything would be the same, only backwards. Pat said I had to stop all these stupid food rules, and Mum said we were a package deal. Like when you buy sausages and the butcher says there's a promotion so you have to get the sweet Thai chili sauce even if you don't like it.

Mum shouted at him in French: '*Vous êtes tous les mêmes!!*' Then Pat said, 'Why do you do that when you know I can't understand?' So Mum said it in Australian: that sometimes the way he talks is blunt like a dull knife. She started to cry and told him the heat in Australia sucked everything dry and made her feel like she couldn't breathe anymore. And that if he couldn't love me for who I was then maybe we'd just go back to Paris. Pat said Mum was an enabler and what I needed was discipline. So while they were shouting I sat on my bed and listened to my *Best of Johnny Farnham* tape on the cassette player. 'Take the Pressure Down'. 'You're the Voice'. The heavy hitters.

Once some real dancers in sky-blue tights gave us a workshop at school. Me and Dean Flanagan did a duet to 'Two Strong Hearts'. We nailed it. But that night I skipped some of the words. Maybe Pat was gonna be just like Dad and everything would be ruined again. When Mum came into my room I lay down and pretended I was asleep. Then it was quiet and I watched the shadows go across my wall when Pat's car reversed out of the driveway. Could hear him all the way down Hooper's Crossing, going over the one-lane bridge, the back way home. Hands gripping the wheel so tight his knuckles were ready to pop through his skin. All 'cause his heart was scared that Mum would leave.

Here in the dam I look across at Pat floating on the water and I know he's been watching the colour fade from the exact same memory. Before either of us can say anything, the sky above fills with hundreds of butter-flies. Like a moving painting changing shape and size in a dance only they know. Me and Pat are puppets with hundreds of tiny strings and the butterflies lift us up towards them, leaving specks of dust on our face as their wings flap in slow motion.

'Dylan, about the boat...'

Pat's words cut the strings and we are back on top of the water. I breathe out and blow those butterflies up higher and higher until they're nothing more than tiny dots fading into the blue sky.

'I need you to listen...'

But I don't want to hear about the boat right now. I don't want to hear or see anything except what's right here. I'm listening to the bush, alive with a sharp endless rhythm. In this dry heat cicadas blare. Crows caw.

'Go on, you know what he has to say,' whispers that dark wolf deep inside my chest. But if Pat tells me about the boat and where we are really going, he might spark a fire. The whole bush might go up, so I duck under the water. Hold my breath until my lungs are about to burst.

17

Bleed 'im dry

Walking out of the dam the breeze makes my nipples stick out like the rubber end of a pencil. I don't have mountains yet, just molehills, but they are there. When Pat sees them he slips in the mud and splutters about. I offer him my hand again but he doesn't want to take it. Gets his pants on real quick then heads off without me.

You know how some people say change is the only constant? Well they've never driven through the middle of nowhere like we are now. My crop top is still damp and it feels nice underneath my T-shirt, flapping in the wind. I look out at miles of nothing but red dirt and it's like we've been travelling just to stay in the same spot. That's the Red Queen theory of evolution. A polar bear changes from brown to white so he can sneak up on prey more easily but at the same time, that snow fox he's after just got faster legs. Like the Red Queen in *Alice in Wonderland* everyone's running just to stay in the same place and I'm scared we'll never make it. Scared that Pat will finally tell me what he's been meaning to since we began the trip. About where we're really going.

Last pub on Pat's run is called The Last Shout and that's no joke. It's the actual last place someone will hear you shout for the next 500 kilometres because after Karalee there is not a single living soul north, east, west or south. Pat says there'd been talk the Last Shout was getting a makeover and goodness knows everyone likes a transformation story. Like Sue-Ellen from Arkansas whose house burnt down in a fire because her pa smoked a handmade pipe in his bedroom, which also had a collection of newspaper cuttings dating back to 1964. To exacerbate matters Sue-Ellen had lost the piggery in her divorce and weighed close to 200 kilograms because she ate her feelings. But then the host with big hair and chipmunk teeth from *Turning around Tragedy* came and built her a new house with a mini-piggery out the back. The show brought a mobile makeover van because there was only a slaughterhouse and fishing store in the town. Couldn't do much about the fatness so they just rolled her into an orange taffeta dress and slapped on some electric pink lipstick. Red carpet was laid down over the muddy driveway and she had to walk past all these people clapping. At the end they gave Sue-Ellen a baby pig with a big red bow tied around its neck.

To cut a long story short the Last Shout had been made over too, with a new pokie room at the back that Pat calls the Shrine. More machines than the Watering Hole in Wanteegi. Rows and rows all blinking and beeping like a puppy dog waiting to be thrown a ball, all saying, 'Look at me, I'm the prettiest, I pay out the most, I can make it all happen, jackpot, jackpot!' Mum said the machines had already taken away her and Pat's future. I don't know how that works if the future is always ahead of you, but she'd said it enough to make me think it was true. The future for her was living with Pat and having the great Australian dream—a house and a dog and a barbeque on Sunday with the men holding tongs and drinking beer while the ladies put out potato salad and tell the kids off when they try to grab a lamington before lunch. Somehow, all that was in the coins he gave to the pokies. And still Pat thought he could break one of those machines in, like a wild brumby only with magic numbers instead of a whip.

'So tell me, do you feel lucky? Well do ya, punk?'

I didn't make that up; it's from a movie about a man who doesn't wash very often. Pat didn't answer, just walked through to the main bar in a trance leaving me to carry the last cardboard-cutout man inside. This one's head accidentally got jammed in the back door and had a crease through his face like a big operation scar. Lawrence the Chinese publican was on the phone. 'Nah, sorry, Joyce. Haven't seen him,' he says, looking at a dopey old man propping up the bar with his elbows. The man slaps a few dollars on the counter and walks out.

I set up the cardboard-cutout man; cap on head, beer in hand. Maybe Pat thought I was the one feeling lucky because he handed me a cup full of ten-cent pieces.

'You think you can hear water? Maybe you can hear money too.' He told me to sit at the back of the room so Lawrence wouldn't see. It's not the legal thing for kids to do and it's against my moral code but I went anyways. Sat at the back of the room all incognito.

That's when I noticed her. She had cold metal running through her veins. Hair pulled back so tight the comb marks left deep lines all the way to her scalp. Her spinal cord stuck out like an old skinny lizard. There was a massive two-litre bottle of Coke on the floor 'cause I guess her insides were so dried up she was always thirsty. I could see the cracks in her lips and dry flakes of skin she kept trying to peel off with her teeth. Cannibalising herself. Eating from the outside in.

She pulls the lever, sucks in her breath and pats the machine five times on the side. Three crowns fall into place and a waterfall of silver coins spills into the tray below. But this was dirty magic and nothing good would come from it.

'Slit-eye Larry reckons he's gonna reel in them rich chinks from China,' she says.

Margie would've said she was cheap and nasty like a two-day-old pastie, jingling coins with her long bony fingers, turquoise nails chipped at the end.

'But maybe I'll just bleed 'im dry instead.'

I think she cast a spell on me, that woman. Her stale breath fills the room with a dirty haze and I can't see much past my hands in front of me. I am going to swell up and suffocate with those words stinging me all over: 'bleed 'im dry'. I also didn't want the chinks from China to come here and lose all their coins because maybe they were a nice family.

Pat is still talking to Lawrence, oblivious to the disaster unfolding behind him, so I go around the back of the machines looking for their power source. The cables and wires are all hooked together with plastic ties that were stored in a broom closet. I put my finger on the switch and wait for someone to yell 'freeze!' But no one does so I flick it. And that's when the witch screams her turkey gobble: I've taken her dirty magic away. Pat knows straight off the bat it is something to do with me. Quick as lightning he pulls me out of the broom closet and glares with those wild, furious eyes. Funny thing is, when Lawrence sees how angry the witch is he smiles at me. She starts jumping up and down shrieking at Lawrence that she'd just hit the $500 jackpot and the money was still coming out. But that is a down-and-out lie. I saw the numbers flashing on her machine and it only said $50. Lawrence is nodding his head while the witch keeps up her fake little hissy fit. Then she lunges at me with her cup of coins like some kind of wild attacking bird.

'This is a crock-a-shit and youse know it! If you can't keep your little Abo in line then I will!' Just like with the white vultures on the bus, I don't think it is the time or place to set things straight. And besides, witches like her don't care. One black is the same as another to them.

Pat steps in front of me so she clobbers him instead, right in the eyeball.

For a quiet man Lawrence sure can shout when he wants. He points at the door and tells the witch to get out.

She cackles and says we've mucked about with the wrong family.

I call after her: 'It's the year of the duck and that's what Pat is, so you can't touch us!'

But she's already gone.

'You're gonna need a lot more than a duck,' says Larry. And Larry was right.

18

I can get you out

I hate it when people ruin a perfectly good name. For example, Amanda Pearson let me fall into the creek during a trust exercise at school camp. Joke was on her because I love getting wet, but I don't trust Amandas now. And even though Tina Arena is a gift to humanity her name has now been soiled for life. Turns out this pokie witch is another Tina and her brother is the one and only cop in town. Darren. Two minutes after she storms out of the pokie room a police car skids into the hotel car park. Darren walks inside like a bow-legged cowboy, pulling his belt up under that big playdough beer gut of his. The wrong Tina's following behind, all smarmy-like. Lawrence steps forward and says he doesn't want to press charges.

'Well, that may be, Larry, but it's not that simple.' Darren smiles like Lawrence has 1.5 brain cells and wears a tea-cosy for a hat.

Pat then sidles up and says HE wants to press charges for assault on account of the swollen eye he is sporting, but it all gets out of hand and soon he's screaming at Darren. Then Tina hits Pat over the head with her pink fluffy handbag, but it's Pat who Darren handcuffs and throws into the back of the paddy wagon! He's a bent copper; bent in all the wrong directions no doubt about it.

So I have to sit in the front seat with him all the way to the station which was so close to the pub I could have walked and got there faster, but I'm guessing big Darren drives everywhere just to show off. He smells like cheap soap. The small little white bars you find in motels that are not even wrapped in paper. And his breath is a brewery, which is illegal because he's supposed to be a teetotaller under the uniform.

'What are you doin' with this fella, luv?'

'Who I keep company with is none of your concern.'

'Everything in this town is my concern.'

This part of the story should be made into a conspiracy movie because it is a pavlova piled high with trouble and nonsense. Darren chucks Pat into the cell down the back of the station and says he'll stay there until the wrong Tina is reimbursed and that in regards to the black eye, well that was a matter of self-defence. Although Pat can't see us, I can see him and he's prowling that cage like an angry bear. I try to burn a hole through the bars with my eyes, turn my anger into a laser beam but I was totally un-super. No special powers at all. Pat gave all his money to the wrong Tina back at the pub to try to smooth things over, and she just pocketed it like nothing ever happened.

'Now the thing I'm trying to figure out is what's goin' on here,' Darren calls out to Pat. He looks me over then turns back to the cell.

'You a kiddy fiddler or what?'

What Pat says is dead rude. Like a swear jar had broken, spilling *&%$##$@% all over the floor. The whole time Darren just watches Pat with a blank face. I get scared when I don't know how to read people.

'You know, I can't abide cursing. It really fuckin' shits me.' And then copper Darren smiles because he is being ironical. His brewery breath floats out of his mouth again and I feel sick.

This is Ghandi's might-over-right for sure. If we want to get to the boat I'll have to take charge of the situation. Like a fox that chews its own paw off to get out of a trap, I'll have to let part of me go too.

When Darren goes to take a piss I scramble over to the cell. Pat's knuckle-popping hands are wrapped around the bars. I look him square in the eyes, through all the fury to the centre. 'I can get you out.'

Pat is yelling after me but I don't look back, not even one time.

•

I saw it as we drove into town. They all look the same, and maybe in a way I'm drawn to the treasures that are waiting inside: all the dreams people thought they could buy back but lost for good. The bell over the door tinkles. It's a friendly yellow sound, makes you feel like you've been there before. I know I have to focus because if I look at anything for too long I'll be in danger of losing my way.

'G'day, luv.'

The man behind the counter's reading the *Trading Post*, drawing perfect circles round things that take his fancy. I rummage around in my bag and hold it in my hand. Close my fingers tight around it and press it into my skin. I feel them coming back, running through my body, like an electric current, those memories. Let them come out of the necklace and into my heart where I can keep them safe.

I can let go because now it is empty of her and what she'd been to me. The man carefully holds it up, looks at all those rainbow moonstones so perfect and round, just like the circles on his paper. And I bet he's wondering why is it called a rainbow moonstone when it's as pale as snow.

'Where'd you go gettin' something like this?'

'It was an air loom. But now it's empty.'

He looks me over and wonders if I'm the real deal or not. 'This yours to sell?'

I nod and we hold each other's gaze. Not sure how he could understand what was going on, but his eyes crinkled up at the sides like my cat had just run away and I was putting up posters hoping someone had found it.

'Yeah. That's the way it goes,' he says.

I don't know if he rips me off like wrapping paper at Christmas but I feel in my bones like a fair and honest deal has been done. I pocket the money and piss bolt back to the police station. Run across the road and get morse-coded by a car swerving to miss me. *BEEP, BE-BEEP, BEEEP!!!*

And then I'm inside again, running through the corridor, sharp turn past the water fountain and up to the front desk where dirty Darren is finishing off a packet of Smith's salt and vinegar chips. The worst flavour of all, of course.

'Oh. We have decided to grace this humble establishment with our presence again.'

Him trying to be a wordsmith won't throw me off my game. I burn through his smarmy smile with a steely glare and run my fingers over the money in my pocket, soft and smooth with a rubber band holding all those notes together. I flick that band one, two, three times over, all while I stare that copper down. Flick, flick, flick.

I don't want to touch Darren in case he stains my soul so I chuck the money on the desk.

'A woman of independent means, are ya?'

Pat yells out, wants to know what's happening, but dodgy Darren is like a kid in the All American Candy Store off Chambers Street, eyes lit up wide like he's got a Babe Ruth bar, four Reese's peanut butter cups and a bag of corn candy all to himself. He takes the rubber band off and slowly flicks through the notes, licking his finger with a slimy goanna tongue.

''Bout eighty bucks short, luv,' he says, smiling. 'Come give us a kiss and we'll call it a day.'

Thinks he's got one over on us.

Pat starts shaking the bars and breaks that swear jar all over again with his &*%$$#@@**&&%$#$@. But quick as lightning that memory-horse bolts through my mind and brings me something useful.

'He saw you, that man across the street.'

'What man?'

'Your neighbour, the one with the wooden leg.'

'What do you know about Prossie Paul?'

I know Darren's neighbour is nicknamed Prossie Paul on account of his *prosthetic limb*. Like false teeth for your legs. And now that copper looks uneasy, knows I'm onto something.

'He took some pictures one time, when you were wearing that dress you said was for Aunty Sue.'

He's got that gobsmacked mouth 'cause I've found his secret.

Everyone knows that dressing up is fun and there's no harm in that. And dresses aren't just for women because men in Scotland and Fiji wear skirts just to get a litre of milk down the shops. So if Gobby McRobby here wants to wear a short lilac number that's fine with me. But Darren's face goes red like an ox-heart tomato, and that uniform he wears so tight and cocky means nothing now. He keeps shaking his head trying to pretend he doesn't know what I'm on about. Fumbles through his keys and opens Pat's cell fast as he can.

'Sick. The both a youse.'

But he never looks us in the eye. Just crawls back into his badge the only way he can.

We make it to the front door but in the reflection of the window I get a shock. Never come face-to-face with a gun before. Darren's hand has gone all gerry-hat-trick and shaky. And his face is pouring with sweat, stains under his armpits too. We are frozen to the spot, don't even want to breathe in case the butterfly effect makes his finger pull the trigger splattering us all over the walls. *Do you feel lucky? Well do ya punk?* Suddenly the phone rings and I'm dead sure Darren's gonna panic.

At the same time a scrawny man with straggly grey hair comes in wanting to know if anyone's found his pet cockatoo, Dolly, who's been gone the best part of a week. It's only then he sees what's going on: the phone ringing off the hook, drongo Darren and his quivering gun and us. Hands half up in the air, feet spread like we've had an unfortunate bowel incident in the middle of the playground. And while this old fella is trying to put it all together in his mind, we piss bolt out of there. I don't know if he ever found Dolly, but sometimes when I see a bunch of cockatoos fly overhead, I think of him and deadbeat Darren decked out in his frilly lavender frock.

19

Creatures below
the surface

Running back to the pub I picture us dodging bullets while Darren shoots at our feet. But the whole street is dead quiet like everyone has packed their bags and left town. Maybe Darren goes troppo every second Tuesday and people have to bunker down just in case there's a shooting spree.

I've never been so happy to see Pat's junkyard of a car. We skid out of town with every body part intact. But then Pat lets loose: 'What was Darren going on about being eighty bucks short and what did lavender frocks have to do with anything?'

When you get out of the crazy, you don't step back inside and pick it apart. You breathe a sigh of relief, say, 'Well that was nuts!' and move on. So I don't say anything. I do wonder where we're gonna sleep tonight, since we were supposed to stay at Lawrence's pub.

'This has done it for sure, you know that?'

I did know. I'd mucked it all up for him and his job. Absconding with droopy-boobed nanas, moving Pat's car into the right car space but the wrong Holden ute, turning off pokies and making witches money hungry. Even though I always have the best of intentions, sometimes my stupid smarts make it all go wrong. Everything feels washed away: a watercolour landscape fading further into the background. Life less real every second we move forward. I don't know anymore about the boat or Mum's spirit. And God, if you are listening, you made me cruel either way—leaving those baby birds in the tree to die or keeping my mum alive. So I'll thank you not to punish me anymore. You win.

Pat pulls over to answer his phone, walks up and down in front of the car kicking the dirt with his boots.

'Yeah, you see…I understand that, but…it was just…this is not…'

And he's pulling faces trying to keep all the shouting he wants to do from going into Ray's ear. At the end he nods, not because he agrees with his boss but because he's given up too. When it gets too hard, sometimes that's just what you have to do. I take out the old letters from my bag. Maybe little-kid Dad kept writing 'cause he thought William would come back if he just asked the same question over and over, believing things could change. But in the very last letter, Dad doesn't ask at all. He's figured out you can't change anything when you're a kid and the only thing you get when you keep asking to be loved, is a bruised heart.

Pat drives as far and long as he can, lips moving silently all the way. Makes me think about homeless Ian who rides the bus all day, then sits in the library reading Indian cooking magazines until they throw him out because he's not even ethnic. Pat is mumbling about the money we've lost. He'd even given the wrong Tina his boot notes—last-resort cash stashed in his left boot. I hope it stank so bad all the currency slid off like that Dali man's melty watch.

The sun rises and sets in the blink of an eye. Now it's dark Pat's bones are tired, aching for a break.

'Why don't we just park ourselves under the stars tonight?' Pat was trying to put a positive spin on poverty, like it would be fun to have a sleep-out. In the middle of the bush full of spiders, snakes and midnight noises that have no name or face. But I know in that moment he needs a sidekick.

'Yeah, that's a great idea, Pat,' I say like I'm going to the circus for the first time.

We make a campfire and chicken noodle cup-a-soup. How do they cook the chicken until it turns into a powder? I sing a Tina Arena medley ('Heaven Help My Heart'—'Chains'—'Wasn't it Good') until I think Pat has gone to sleep. But the fire has drawn him back

143

into the past. It'll do that if you stare into it for long enough.

'He used to dangle me over the water, just let me hang there. Couldn't have been more than a scrawny four and Stu was twelve but you wouldn't bat an eyelid if he said sixteen. And I could see the shadows of all these creatures below the surface, all these sea monsters coming up from the bottom to grab me with their mouths full of jagged teeth. Said he didn't mean no harm, but he did. Called our sister chubby checkers and she still takes those diet pills, always a fat little eight-year-old. He made people feel shit 'cause he felt shit about himself, ya see?'

Thought Pat might throw his head back and howl at the moon. Not just for all that stuff in the past. He is sorry for something that hasn't happened yet.

'It's not a colour that makes you do bad things,' he says. 'It's something deep down inside.'

Pat stokes the fire and tiny embers dance through the air. I want to open up my chest and back-burn the black so the badness inside of me never gets a chance to grow. But I just wriggle into my sleeping-bag and watch those embers float higher and higher into the sky. Night-time in the bush is a loud kind of quiet. Crickets and nocturnals scampering around with their night-vision eyes on. But it isn't just the animals. The air is filled with Pat's other memories trying to be heard.

Some fall into the fire, they screech out with pain as they die. Others make a run for it hoping Pat will forget about them all together. One of them dances over the fire and flickers into my dreams.

Pat's a boy no more than seven. It's a good day to be proud; he's been chosen. By God, no less. New clean shirt and a blue tartan tie. It's hard to get the knot right, but important things take time. Pat cocks his head. Feels nice to have his dad so close without the smell of whisky on his breath and a cutting hand across the cheek. 'Up and under, pull it tight.' Makes it seem so easy. He takes a step back and says, 'Smart, you are.' And smart Pat feels. Mum's not coming, that nerve in her back is pinched again and she's on the couch, hand on her tummy like she's trying to stop the pain from moving. But she's made a cake, tells Pat to take it with him. There'll be a special morning tea. What about Stu? He's nowhere to be seen, more like a boarder than a brother. Maybe Pat and his dad will make a special day of it, get a pie on the way home. But when they pass the doggies his dad nips inside: 'Gotta drop something off to a mate real quick.' Pat thinks nothing of it because today he's called into God's service and taken into his care. Sits on the kerb and waits. And then he realises his dad's not coming back. It's not even race day but there's always something going on inside. Blokes to see, bets to be lost and won. Monies owed collected, one way or another. So he walks to church himself. Peers in the window but can't bear to go in alone. No one to place a hand on his shoulder with sentimental pride.

Pat legs it to the park round the corner, sits on the bench and opens the cake tin. He breaks a piece off and shoves it into his mouth, trying to let the sweetness take all the pain away. But it can't cause he's only seven and the world is unforgiving when you hurt like this. He leaves that cake on the bench and sits on a swing. Watches a swarm of seagulls scamper over and soon there's only a mess of crumbs left. Pat pushes himself higher, higher, hoping that God will reach down out of the clouds and take him anyway. Just as he is.

New days don't wipe the slate clean. Come morning, embers in the pit are still glowing under the grey powdery ash and I'm glad I didn't jump into the fire, watch my skin melt together like the top of hot milk. Pat's already awake, staring at me hard. For a moment all I see is that little boy pushing himself higher towards the sky.

'Do you believe in God?' I ask.

'No matter what they tell you, we're not all the same in his eyes. Some are chosen, some get left behind.'

I know that's the end of that, 'cause he's still thinking about what I'd done to get him out of jail. Some people say they have eyes on the back of their head but only so little kids don't cause trouble. Pat has eyes on his ears. Even though he couldn't see me pay dirty Darren, he'd heard me throw that bundle of money down on the desk. Even though we came from different family trees Pat was suffering from a kind of guilt only someone who shares blood can. Even though he'd cursed me under his breath a million times, we'd been threaded into each other's story with the same needle.

'You should'na done that. I can't get it back. I just can't.'

You know that snazzy toy some businessmen put on their desks to help them think? The row of silver balls suspended from thin wires? You pull the first ball back and let go, watch as the energy passes through and pushes the last one up in the air, then back again. Tap, tap, tap. That's me and Pat. Pushing each other into the past and back again, just to slow the future down because we're both scared of what's to come. Bad things can suddenly happen. Time and love are always being lost and you can't do anything about it. That's how the wolf got inside of me: found a big gaping hole just waiting to be filled. I'd been lying to myself about where I am going. But only because I know it is going to tear me and Pat apart when we finally get there.

20

Trickling through the cracks

Next morning we sit in the McDonald's car park eating our egg-and-bacon McMuffin. The girl had to cut it in half 'cause Pat only had enough coins for one. And a coffee; he has to have a coffee with milk and three sugars to kickstart his heart.

'Dylan, you're old enough to know that sometimes things don't work out like you planned. So we gotta set things straight.'

Well fancy that. When it suits him, I'm too young to understand the lay of the land and the ways of the world, but now I've evolutionised enough to be let down, turned around and gutted like a fish.

'It's my birthday today,' I say which isn't true but when my head gets overheated with emotions I say it is and people usually forget why they were being mean or selfish or rude. Besides, I have a right in and outside of the law to be angry with Pat for what he is about to say.

'I didn't mean to let it get this far without telling you. But…the way you see things is complicated.'

The only thing I see is how spineless Pat has become, shifting blame instead of owning it. There's a little river of runny egg moving south down Pat's chin and he wipes it off with a napkin. Then, he folds the napkin as many times as he can.

Finally, he says, 'What you imagine and what exists in real life are not always the same thing.'

I thought E.T. would come and visit me when I was ten just like the boy in the movie, and for my whole year of being nine I was so excited about turning into double digits. But he never came. So maybe Pat is a little bit right.

'Dylan, you know when your mum went in the ground, she had to stay there. She can't come out.'

I should have built a net with my words to stop Mum from falling: 'I love you bigger and further than the moon, beyond time and past all eternity.' But I said nothing. Heard the snap of her neck as it broke. Dead just like that.

'There *is* no boat,' Pat says. 'You know there never was.'

I slap him hard across the cheek. Crack like a whip and it's stinging red! He sucks his breath in fast, not quite believing I could do such a thing. Everyone wants the dream world to be real and the real world to be a dream. If you don't then you're lying. But when the worlds collide everything all falls apart.

I get out of the car and run towards the bush.

'*Maman, arrête!*'

I want to change the story and choose another path; turn the wheels and cogs around again. Please, don't leave me with him.

But then I stop dead in my tracks. It covers the sky, light as a feather. On a forty-one-degree day in the middle of Australia, snow is falling. And if that isn't a miracle, I don't know what is. I open my mouth and wait until a single flake lands on my tongue. So cold it feels hot, melts away quick into water. I swallow that little peace offering. No matter how many times grief cuts into my heart Mum saves me again. Spinning my arms round and round, the paddocks in the distance disappear under a blanket of white.

I step outside of my body and watch from afar. Watch as my skin sheds, falling to the ground behind me in strips like bark. Laid bare, the truth rises to the surface. A smaller version of Dylan crawls into the backseat of the car and lies down, legs tucked up to her chest trying to become even smaller. She puts herself to sleep under the longest of spells hoping that when her eyes open she'll be back in Beyen. The bumps in the gravel road soothe like a lullaby and heavy eyes sink to the back of my skull.

•

Two hours pass in a second and I jolt awake with wind fresh on my face like cold tap water in the morning. But this air has salt on its back. It's a sea breeze. We've found the water. Not just a dirty puddle by the side of the road or a fifteen-second sunshower. But the source of all magic, wonder and imagining you can ever know. It creeps over me like a big tribe of ants, tingling and pinching my new skin. And then there's a low sounding buzz in my ears, slowly building as it brings me closer.

We're driving the coastline, weaving along the water like a sea snake. The bushy windbreakers clear away and then I have it. People always remember the first time they tried cheese fondue or heard Eddy Grant's 'Electric Avenue' because they are both life-changing experiences. But do you remember the first time you saw the sea? The first time you heard waves tumbling over each other up the sand before rolling back into the ocean's sun-scorched belly?

The sea pierces my heart with joy that day, stains it with a happiness so deep I wonder if we'd all been baptised and born again. But I'm lost and found at the same time. That joyful heart of mine is bled dry by betrayal when we turn the corner. Away from the water. Into suburbia, and down a quiet street lined with weatherboard houses pretending to be pretty.

Then I see them. Standing on the footpath like they are waiting for a late bus. My chest burns as that wolf inside of me howls with laughter. He's been waiting for this moment the entire trip. 'You can't run from what you are, you silly, stupid girl!'

I want to tear him out of my body.

'Dylan, you need to be brave right now. That's all you need to do,' says Pat.

No, no, no. This is a state of emergency. Immediate evacuation required. I spin the steering wheel and the tyres lose their grip. For a moment I think we're gonna crash into the rubbish bins ahead, but Pat grabs the wheel and we swerve back onto the road.

We're stopped dead in the middle with our bodies lurching back like the end of a rollercoaster ride.

'This is where you belong. They're your family too,' Pat says, trying to get his breath back. And up they come, running in the rear-view mirror with eyes wide open, flapping their arms around trying to get to me.

I'm willing the car to transform into an impenetrable metal beetle that flies away. How can strangers be your family? He's blackety black, wearing a cardigan and thick glasses. I look at the brown woman's eyes and there's my dad, the way she's squinting and chewing on her bottom lip at the same time. The other one is blonde like Mama, but has her hair cut short, shaved on one side. Margie would say she should know better than to play with an asset like that. Each woman has a small arm wrapped around her lower leg, like an octopus tentacle.

A little face pokes out between them, dark eyes glaring at me from under a mop of brown curly hair. Even though his mouth is shut tight I know he's laughing at me. I want to scream at them all: 'Stop looking at me! Can't you see I'm invisible?'

Maybe I don't want to be real after all. If I was a machine, then I wouldn't be afraid like I was gonna pee my pants again, or worse. Pat's spun a web of lies so far and wide I don't know when it started or where it will end. I want to bust out of the car, run so fast they can only watch me vanish over the hill and say, 'We lost her.'

All I can hope for is some divine intervention delivering me from evil. By the time I grab the doorhandle he is already there, peering in at me. Funny thing, his eyes are full of fear too. I can see through them and back to myself.

All this time believing my way to an imaginary boat only to end up in the middle of a crazy snotstorm because Pat is a gutless wonder. He winds down the window and mumbles to the old man who has walked around to his side. The old man nods and walks back to his house with the others.

And then Pat parks the car at the side of the road. 'Dylan. I'm gonna sit in this car with you, and when you're ready we can go and meet your family together. That's your Grandad William, your Aunty Cecilia and well…I don't know about the others.'

I'm not listening. I just want to hurt Pat like he's done to me.

'Mum didn't love you. She never did.'

'Don't say that.'

'Black men are trouble. You should know better.'

'Like I told you, Dylan, it's something deep inside that makes people do bad things, not a colour.'

Pat pretends this is a natural conclusion to the trip. Like it was always gonna be this way.

'This is your house now. And your mum would be real proud of you.'

'You're a liar! You never said anything about him, not even once!'

That dark colour is rising in the back of my head like a tornado, ripping up my memories and good thoughts about the world. The wolf has won.

I wind the window down, smash my snow globe on the road and stare at all the little splintered pieces of glass lying on the ground. The water trickles through the cracks and soon enough only tiny white specks of snow are left. I've carried it safely all the way from Beyen and now all that precious care means nothing.

21

The wardrobe revolt

It is dark in the wardrobe and not like the one at home that smelt of Anais Anais perfume and soft cotton dresses that floated down from above like weeping willows onto my face. This one smells like mould and wrongness, and there's a crack in a floorboard waiting to split in two. There are no fur coats so I can't escape into Narnia, even though I want so bad to be having tea and crumpets with those friendly beavers. Fat lot of good that metal fish has done me. Of all the times and places I needed it to come good, and nothing. Maybe Dad is in on the joke. I can't repel, reject, reverse or rewind anything now. Especially not in this dark wooden box I've found myself in. I hold the fish in my hand, running the top of my fingertips across the scales and wonder how I can get back to the car without being noticed.

I'd run into the house because there was movement at the station. Only primitive people squat wherever they are, so I went inside the house like it was the library toilet. When I finished I saw them all talking about me in the kitchen. That small boy was sitting under the table, just like I used to do at home. Rubbing some grubby soft toy against his dry lips. He looked to the door and ogled me. My cheeks burned and I shouted at them all like a wild banshee: 'I'M NOT HERE!'

I stormed off to the front door but it was locked (what a surprise) so I ran from room to room until I found one with a vase of flowers on the desk, a bed and a wardrobe. I jumped inside and hugged my knees, waiting for everyone to forget that I was there. But of course this supposed family of mine were infiltrating my human right to freedom, so that was never going to happen.

And sure enough I hear those creaky floorboards drilling into my ears as they enter the room and stand in front of the wardrobe.

'She doesn't like runny eggs. And watch your taps because she likes water. I've written you a list. Oh, and the forks.'

That's Pat telling them all about my habits, which is just rude because you're not supposed to talk about someone if they are there, even if they're inside a wardrobe.

I peer out of the little keyhole and see William hobbling onto one knee, and then squinting back at me. He shouts like I'm at the bottom of a well with a bucket on my head: 'You want a fork, Dylan?' He flaps his hand at Aunty Cecilia and she races out the door. I hear a clunking, crashing sound and then *doof doof doof* as she runs back.

'There's more in the sink we can wash.' She's a bit breathless.

William holds the fork up in front of the wardrobe. I peer a little harder and can see his hand shaking. But I still don't open the door, so he puts it down on the floor.

'We'll always have cutlery for you, Dylan.' William's voice is a little bit gravelly like he's either about to cry or has biscuit crumbs in his throat.

The little gremlin appears again. I hear someone call him Joni. He's wearing gumboots that are too big for his feet and he stumbles a little before steadying himself. Puts a teaspoon down next to the fork. Typical. Small, clumsy and clueless. This kid is obviously not related to me.

'Well, how 'bout we let Dylan get used to her... wardrobe,' says that William Freeman.

Everyone leaves because they know I am revolting. That's what the French do, because they won't stand for nonsense and they always march through the streets singing angry songs about when tomorrow comes.

I'm travelling back in my mind to when Pat was making all those phone calls back in Beyen, saying they were none of my beeswax, and I put all the pieces together like a jigsaw. Now I know Pat had been talking to William, figuring out this whole plan to dump me here because I'm just excess baggage to him. Through the peephole I can see they're in the hallway mumbling in low voices, all sombrous (serious and sombre), and then William hands Pat a big wad of cash. Human trafficking pure and simple. I'd been transported halfway across the country like sheep on a ship to the Middle East. At least the sheep got to go on a boat, but my journey ends here. No one had ever asked about where and who I wanted to be now that Mum wasn't here.

Forty-seven minutes pass by. I am waiting it out. Some people stay in the wardrobe for decades and it's not until they're thirty-four that cousin Gracie says, 'Aaron's *finally* come out of the closet.'

I should have brought a choc-chip muesli bar with me. The house is too quiet. Maybe if I scream the silence would fall out the window. Slowly I push one of the wardrobe doors open and slip out. Creep over to the window where I can see Pat sitting in the car. Just staring straight ahead like he's caught in some kind of trance. I don't see his eyes blink, not even one time. And even though he has a house to go back to (if the repo men haven't chucked it on the back of their truck), he doesn't want to leave.

Home is only a space full of emptiness that can't be filled even if you buy a pot plant from Bunnings to liven up the living room or turn up the volume on the TV. No matter how loud or colourful the distraction you're still alone. He is sitting with his shame like when people throw word-stones at you. *Abo, nigger, coon, monkey*, leaving little puncture marks all over your skin. Even though I partly hate him, other parts (mostly my ankles) want to run outside and chuck the car keys in the drainpipe to keep Pat here a little longer.

The only company I'm keeping is a hungry stomach. I can hear pots banging, oil sizzling and now the smell molecules are floating under the door. I'm pretty sure it's chicken, and that's hard to deny.

When I open the door there are seven forks waiting for me on the floor. Long, heavy metal grooves, pretty flower patterns, ridges around the handle and a green plastic one for picnics. I stand at the door to the kitchen and watch that polite kind of eating people do just moving food around the plate. The boy is asleep on the couch with a blanket over him, scrunched in on himself like a small turtle. I still don't know who the woman with shaved hair is. William nods in her direction as he talks to Pat.

'Jules here works right near that chicken factory on Hurst Street. They've got a direct outlet.' He gets up and opens the freezer door. The whole thing is filled with plastic bags. Like a poultry morgue.

'She keeps bringing me the whole bird even though—'

'—you're a leg man, we know, Bill,' replies Jules, like she's heard it a hundred times before. They're all laughing now. Nothing funny about frozen chicken parts.

William catches me standing in the doorway and quick as a flash his smile fades. He races back over to the table and lifts up a plate.

'There's still dinner here for you.'

Some French stumbles out of my mouth 'cause I want them to hear me but not understand. The translation is roughly like this: 'You are all dirty and dangerous, and in the morning I am running away because no way are you my family.'

'That's pretty, sweetheart,' says Jules the chicken woman.

William says that Jules is Joni's other mum. I think what a good idea that is, because men stink out the bathroom and say thoughtless things, so if there were just two ladies in the house it would smell very sensitive and clean. I ask if they are both hermaphrodites to get a baby. I thought it was a very sensible medical question but everyone burst out laughing and that Joni boy just kept staring at me with those glassy eyes of his and that ratty-looking soft toy.

Cecilia says that Jules's brother Abe helped her make a baby. He lives in Brisbane so he is just an uncle to Joni.

Jules says I can come and have arvo tea at their house whenever I like. She's a lighter shade of safe, but I can't afford to trust anyone right now, so I grab my plate and go sit back in the wardrobe listening to the cutlery as it echoes round the kitchen. It's prickly on my ears and sounds like the exact moment my snow globe shattered all over the bitumen.

Even though the chicken drumstick is filling that hungry hole in my stomach, there are tears in my eyes and I cannot taste it at all.

22

Painting myself outside in

I stay in that wardrobe the whole night. Don't brush my teeth or even change my clothes. At 10.37 pm Pat comes in and gives me a blanket, says that we'll talk about things in the morning, but I'm not gonna talk about things with him ever again. Everyone is my enemy and everything has gone pear-apple-and-banana-shaped. Three times during the night (11.34 pm, 12.12 am and 1.49 am) I hear William creaking his way through the house with his old bones to peer in on me, checking to see if I have gone weak and nodded off. But not on my watch, no way, no how, no where. Who knows what dark strangers are likely to do in the middle of the night when you are floppy and unconscious. I just breathe extra hard so William thinks I am asleep then he totters back down the hall. He takes ages to close the door trying to be quiet and only ends up making triple the noise. But his fussing about distracts me from my revolting and I fall asleep at 2.06 am. I think.

Long fingers of sunlight creep through the keyhole and underneath the wardrobe door to remind me I'm not alone. Can't blame it for trying, even though company's not always what you want. Cecilia went home after dinner, and so I just have William and Pat to deal with. Breakfast time and they just keep gawking.

I point my finger at William. 'Don't look at me.'

'I'm not looking at you.'

I shoot my finger across to Pat. 'Or you.'

'No one's looking,' says Pat, the perpetual liar.

'All this is a bit new. Gonna take a bit of getting used to,' William says in his gravelly old-man voice.

Ha. What they don't know is that I'm not getting used to *anything* because I am running away. After I have some Vegemite toast and Rice Bubbles.

William pours Pat a cup of tea and his hand is wobbling again like his insides are made of jelly.

'Sorry, milk's off.'

Typical. With all his trembling he's forgotten to turn the milk on. What kind of people are they?

But then Pat puts on a pretend interested face like there's a light bulb glowing above his head. 'Maybe you can help William get some more milk, Dylan.'

Pat writes out a list of all the foods I like including

fish fingers, cheese sticks, barbecue shapes, red not green apples, spaghetti with cheese and butter, never beans from a can, but tinned peaches for dessert. I am going along with it because driving to the shops might become part of my escape plan. Then Cecilia comes and picks us up. At least that kid's disappeared.

Pat says he's coming but at the last minute takes another call from his boss and he starts that pacing of his up and down on the front lawn. I'm still fuming from all his trickery so I don't let him know that this might be the last time we see each other. I just look at him and on the inside of my mind I say, 'Well, that's that.'

All the way into town Aunty Cecilia says how Joni has been waiting for me to come. That he's a quiet little kid but she can tell he's excited to finally have his cousin here. Cousin. I've never been anything to anyone younger than myself. Cousins are supposed to do fun stuff together like go on adventures with peanut-butter sandwiches, hard-boiled eggs and apples wrapped in a tea towel, and discover secrets in the wild that grown-ups don't know about. Can't do that with a silent rug rat like Joni. Cecilia hums along to a song on the radio. This is a stupid town to live in because not once, not even one single time did they play Tina Arena or John Farnham. Not even 'Take the Pressure Down', which is a classic in anyone's book.

There is only a Woolworths supermarket, not a Coles, not even an IGA run for the locals by the locals. And everything looks different, even the footpath is a wet slug shade of grey. There's no public statue in the town square and right now I miss that hand, back in Beyen. On hot days, curling up inside and pushing against the hard, shiny metal until you feel the heat sink into your back. The only thing I feel now is my stomach drop, like I've swallowed a stone.

William buys me a Golden Gaytime and I eat it because I keep my manners even when I'm rebelling. The fish fingers are a different brand called Timmy's Fish Logs and only came in a packet of twenty not forty like the bulk home-brand pack Mum used to get. Maybe that is a good thing because there isn't much room left in the freezer with all those chicken pieces. Cecilia takes my hand and leads me to aisle eight, which has soap and handwash and bandaids and toothpaste.

'Sweetheart, you just tell me what kind you use.'

She pointed to the *hygiene products* for women: colourful packages of pads and the small white rockets you shoot up your clacker. I know because I peeped through the bathroom door once and saw Mum doing it. There was a string that hung down out of her vajayjay like a little mouse's tail. She wiped up a drop of blood from the ground and flushed it down the toilet. I stared at that spot for weeks after, thinking again how come women don't die when they lose it all—blood magic and magic blood.

I tell Cecelia that my 'little friend' must have got lost, because she still hadn't come to visit. (Maybe that's why I'm still alive.) Cecelia looks real worried and says we might have to go to the lady doctor. I say maybe I'm like the Virgin Mary and I'll have a baby one day without all the hoo-ha. Cecelia buys me a bulk packet of pads just in case I end up not being a miracle.

Funny when you get something in your head like babies, you see them everywhere. Three in aisle eight and a pregnant cashier who looked too old to be. Then while we're stuck in traffic on the way home I look over at a woman in the car four down and across. Straight away I'm travelling inside her memories—swimming through words so heavy they cannot be spoken. For some reason she can't have babies and now it's the only thing that matters. Her clock keeps ticking as she waits and worries that it's all too late. She'd know how I am feeling, how you could miss someone you would never see again (or even meet).

I decide to make a break for it. Traffic light's still red so I bolt out of the car and run down the road, darting in-between cars to get to the empty-womb lady. Jump in the back seat and close the door.

'Jesus! What are you doing?'

I want to say there are lots of other babies in the

world she can have, whose mothers are already in the ground or do not have enough food for them, babies that are crying in an orphanage because there is no one to hold them in the night. But I don't say this because she starts screaming. Then the light turns green and people behind her beep their horns.

'I haven't got any money,' she says with a quiver in her voice like William's trembling hand.

'Neither have I!'

Now all the noises are talking over the top of each other and I'm losing my invisibility. I want to get out and am glad (I admit it) when William opens the back door. 'I'm sorry, madam, I'm so sorry,' he says to the lady.

If you get swallowed by chaos look for detail—let it suck up the noise. When William holds out his hand I look at it closely. His fingers are long and narrow and the skin is rough with rivers of veins cutting this way and that. But I take that hand and when he squeezes it around mine I feel how soft his palm is, warm like a hot-water bottle. And I go with him because in that moment my heart says it is safe to.

Back in Cecilia's car, she yells at me and crunches the gears something chronic 'cause people were beeping her as well.

'You can't do that, Dylan! That was a really dangerous thing to do!'

I was human-trafficked back to William's house with stupid fish logs and plain crinkle-cut chips 'cause there were no barbecue shapes. Not even pizza flavour. And wouldn't you know it, as soon as we get back Cecilia marches inside and is shouting at Pat demanding to see my doctor files. Before I retreat to my room I shout at her: 'MY BLOOD MAGIC IS NOT YOUR BUSINESS!'

Through the wardrobe I can hear her saying bad things to Pat about Mum.

'She was supposed to bring Dylan here. Dad sat in the car park for two hours waiting! And she never showed! Nothing!'

Well, I don't know anything about that. Maybe Mum had accidentally driven to another car park and maybe we had been sitting there waiting too!

'So it's only when there's no other choice, huh? Then suddenly it's all about family?' Cecilia's voice goes up at the end of her sentences.

'She lost her mum! That's all I know. That's all there is for her right now,' says Pat.

'Juliet made her afraid of who she is!' cries Cecilia.

'Your brother did that!' Pat wishes he could pull those words back on a string and shove them into his top pocket.

Even though he's swirling a glass of whisky in his hand, William says, 'How about some tea?' And then there's nothing but the sound of a soft whistle, slowly climbing higher as the water boils. Tinkle, tinkle of teaspoons in the cups. And everyone is just sipping away, taking their thoughts out the window, over the back fence out and down to the sea where they blow far out of sight.

Dinner is strange and all awkward. Pat tells me off for eating all the mash and leaving the peas.

That's not mucking around, that's having *an established order to proceedings*. 'White before green,' I say to Pat. 'You should know that, you're like thirty times older than me.'

But Pat says I can't behave like that anymore. I can feel a tear creeping up but I hold tight, shield my eyes from everyone with my left hand and start to stab the peas with my fork. Those poor little buggers, caught in the crossfire.

Then William clears his throat and says sometimes he likes to eat dessert before mains because he has a sweet tooth.

'Which one?'

He opens his mouth and points way up the back. I see gold in there too.

'Well, I've got five sweet teeth,' I say. And I do: one up top and four down the bottom.

Pat's staying one more night before he heads home to what's left of his job and house. His whole life's turned into a runny egg heading south. After I have eaten the cheap imitation fish logs Cecilia says that things have been difficult for everyone on account of my dad and all the problems he caused. Other people will visit during the school holidays and then I'll see what a nice big family I'm a part of. But she doesn't get it, none of them do. How I look is not who I am. None of these strangers can see past the skin I'm in. I must have been dreaming when I saw it all fall off my body like strips of bark. Now I'll have to do it for real.

3 am. I stick the photo of me and Mum sitting in the Beyen hand onto the bathroom mirror, her beautiful silky-smooth white skin, hazelnut freckles that dot her nose. My skin is a lie.

In the laundry through the other bathroom door I find all these tins of paint under the sink. The brushes are hard and dry. I take the smallest one. It's scratchy but I use it to paint my hands the colour Mum gave me. The paint smells strong like a hospital or factory and makes me feel dizzy when I breathe it in.

Stroke, stroke, rectify, stroke. I hold my hands up to the mirror. They look like gloves, like I'm just playing dress-ups. My heart sinks, this is not how I feel or who I am. Silly girl.

I look at Mum in the photo and she's still smiling at me even though I feel strange in my head. Suddenly a tiny drop of water drips from the tap into the basin. Travelled through all those underground pipes from Beyen, just to comfort me. I put a finger on the rim of the tap and another drop of water slips out onto the tip of my white, gloved finger. I'm listening to the night through that tiny drop of water. The animals outside are calling me: bats, possums, night owls too. I ask them, 'What do you see? Do you see the white girl trapped inside of me?' They sit in the palm of my hand and the drops of water from the sink start singing them a lullaby. The song drops turn into one big ball of light and drift into the air, glowing a night-time yellow, floating higher and higher until they touch the roof. They're trying to get out so I open the window and watch as the ball of light floats away on its own melody. The night air hits me in the face and cools down that strangeness hovering behind my eyes.

Mama, Mama, who am I really? Only you know for sure. I can see it in your smile, in the photo.

The bathroom door opens and Pat comes in. At first he only sees my white, gloved hands but then he says, 'Dylan,' and reaches out slowly. When he touches my arm he knows it is not a dream and that I am still there under my whiteness, still flesh and blood.

'Dylan, where do you go? In your head?'

A million miles away. Where I am in the middle, not on the side or way behind at the back of the line like I am in everyone else's world being squished into a space that doesn't fit.

Pat doesn't have any more words of his own. They've all gone, spinning around his head filled with a why, why, why that is written all over his face. I know that Pat has to take the paint off me now. And that it will hurt. He blinks the tears from his eyes and finds some other bottle below the sink. He puts some of the stinky liquid onto a face cloth and rubs the white off my hands, making messy streaks as he goes. And every touch says sorry, for the things he cannot change.

I stop pretending, because he's seen me inside out. I knew all along we'd be damaged goods by the end of our time together. And now it's come because Pat is going.

We'll be in different worlds when the morning comes and he will drive through night after another night hoping to forget what he has done and how he saw me trying to find my way out of the blackness. He thinks if *he* can just get back, something will finally crawl out of his mouth like a wailing cow that has been hit by a truck and left by the side of the road, a hurting that has been hidden under his tongue all this time. He wants to lock himself away and let that wave of loneliness ride through him once and for all. Because sometimes the only person you can be with is yourself.

23

Cutting the cord

There are different birds here, with new songs. Could be they're showing off but I think they're just happy to have such a fine voice and beautiful morning melody to share. Magpies are the same wherever you go—hungry for worms and loud about life. They're warbling it to me: 'No time to sleep, can you see what a day we've found for you? Sun with not a cloud in the sky so how 'bout it? Up and Adam.'

What they're really offering is a distraction from the night before, but as soon as I sit up and look outside it all comes back.

'Don't sing. I have to remember,' I say and so the magpies stop.

Pat put me to bed after cleaning the paint off my hands. Tucked me in and asked if I was warm enough. I was hot but I didn't say that, just so he would keep fussing about. He leaned close and whispered that he's not strong enough for what I need him to be. Brushed the hair off my face and kissed me on the middle of my forehead. I don't know why but I closed my eyes when he did.

Maybe I wanted to remember what I felt, not what I saw in those last moments. I don't understand why you have to be strong to look after someone. Mum was as soft as a summer peach. We'd cuddle in the hammock under the verandah and I'd lean myself back into her, take her arms and wrap them round me, head resting in the crook of her arm. Sometimes it felt like we were already on our boat rocking back and forth as we sailed across the sea, letting the waves navigate while we slept.

I know, even though I might have said the opposite, that Pat is all bark and no bite. I could have worked things out with his boss, smoothed things over like caramel. 'Look here,' I'd say, resting an elbow on Ray's desk like we go way back. 'Pat's a good egg, a top bloke, straight shooter, diamond in the rough. Bottom line, Ray'—I'd be leaning in here, staring him straight in the eye with my truest words yet—'he's a keeper.' But now I wouldn't be able to explain to Ray that most of the glitches during the trip were my fault because I hadn't read the signs right. I couldn't explain to Ray that crossed wires sometimes wrap themselves around me and make trouble.

I'd tried to tell Pat it could be different now we were by the sea, so wide and deep and full of the right kind of magic that could heal him a little bit, but it was too late. So now we are fractured. Cracked right down the middle and you can't patch something like that together again.

While I appreciate the birds trying to distract me this morning, I'm even more of a loner in the world than I was the day before and have to sigh and groan when I get out of bed. I watch the tiny little pieces of dust in the light. Do they think about anything at all when they float through the air? I wonder if I'll ever see that Pat O'Brien again.

Old people are loud and you can't tell them to tone it down because then you're the rude one. William is banging and crashing around with pots like he's in a hotel kitchen and has no idea where anything goes. There's a whole lot of frozen chicken pieces near the stovetop. William looks up as he chucks them into a big pot.

'I remember one winter back in my university days, I woke up—bitter cold it was—and found a rat on my front doorstep. Frozen solid. The cat had left it there as a present. Can you imagine that?'

I really can't so I just pour myself some Rice Bubbles and focus on the *snap, crackle, pop*. This is difficult because then William starts talking to himself, diluting my powers of concentration.

'Now, do I let them thaw?' He looks up at me again like I care. 'Thought I'd do a casserole, make some room in the freezer for your fishy fingers.'

'They're called Timmy's Fish Logs.'

'Okay.' William smiles and lights the cooker. There's one single rice bubble on the floor. I step on it just to make a mess. Maybe I'm becoming a delinquent. With my French heritage, perhaps I could upgrade to an anarchist or a revolutionary before the week was out. See how William likes having me around then— marching down the street waving a flag singing my freedom songs.

I can hear the moon sending waves in and out round the corner, down the bend, up a hill and through the dunes. It's saying, 'Why are you there when you could be here?'

Maybe I should just let myself be wrapped up in the cold, deep water. But there is something caught. Like a loose thread hooked on a splintered doorway. And then I think that maybe I'm scared. I've never been close to the sea before and when you want something that much it can frighten you. When it's finally there, the whole thing is bigger than you thought and too much to take in. What if the moon pulls the waves so far back it all disappears over the horizon, swallowed up by the setting sun?

I tell William about the black man in the middle of nowhere. 'Did you send him?'

'No, I didn't,' he says, stirring those chicken bits. He's looking deep into that pot and he tells me it doesn't work like that. Not all black people know each other and what a silly idea that is to start with.

Of course he's gonna deny it. That's what guilty people do: 'I never saw him before in my life, Judge! Honest ta God.'

I stay in my room for the next few days and write letters of complaint even though I don't know where to send them. Wednesday's letter is devoted entirely to fruit and hairs. William only has tinned fruit salad and I don't think that fruit should come in small squares. Also he's got really long white nose hairs and I have to sit on my hands to stop myself from pulling them out. By the time Friday comes around I am really in the swing of it and I write a letter to William himself:

Dear William,

You are not me and I am not you. Dad stole my whiteness and you are his father so the buck stops here.

Mum had sunlight under her skin. She was the colour of an angel and sometimes when she stood in front of the window her blonde hair would glow. The only light I've got left is in the palms of my hands and the soles of my feet. That's why I can't get into heaven. Who's ever seen a black angel? My wings would be made of metal and I'd fall out of the sky.

I mostly want to be like Tina Arena when I grow up. I can close my eyes and frown with immense pain. Good singing has to hurt. And when people are sad they need someone to sing the sorrow away.

I did that once to my cat Ashtray who'd gotten himself run over. He was still breathing but all broken and twisted like he was trying to look back at his tail, making little breaths in & out, in & out. I held Ashtray and sang Johnny's 'Burn for You'. I sang away his sorrow. Then Mum took him to the vet and she was crying even though she hated it when Ashtray crawled under the house and howled like he was crazy wild. The vet turned him into ash, which is ironical. But the point is I think I'd be a very good singer in Paris, because they have lots of cats there.

Yours in disrespect,
Dylan.

All this time William's been in the old wooden bungalow out back hunched over these cardboard boxes. He comes out, lights up a cigarette and leans against the door watching all the smoke float up into the air. What are the chances? William gently tapping his ash into a saucer on the window ledge while I'm writing about Ashtray being turned into ash. He looks up at me, startled out of his smoko and quick as a flash I'm inside one of his memories.

There's a sizzling sound like sausages in the pan, only it's skin that's burning. There's my dad. He's the same age I am now but already he's full of fury. Dad takes William's cigarette, holds down his arm and burns him with it, and then he walks away like nothing's happened. I'm going past that moment now. Back, way back. William's holding his newborn son, rocking him softly to sleep. My dad is just a baby, and William has hopes and worries for him in equal measure, sure he's the most precious creature God's blessed anyone with yet. Way back then he is afraid *for* him, not *of* him. Quick as I see his story it's gone.

William stubs the memory out, blows one more mouthful of smoke into the air and goes back inside the bungalow. Through the door I see boxes full of paper and old files in manila folders. William leans over the desk writing notes and ticking off scribbles he's made. Maybe he's a spy for another government. Like Nigeria. They're always trying to get money in and out of the country. I keep one eye closed so he can only see me half as well. But even though he doesn't look up he can tell I am there.

'It always catches up with you. Spend your life dealing with other people's paperwork and forget about your own. Until you retire,' says William.

Mum used to say you should never make decisions when you're emotional and I was both angry and sad so I threw the letter in the bin. Besides, it was mostly about cats and Paris and not really about how I felt. But then my hands start acting on their own and before I can stop, they're rummaging around in my backpack.

I walk into the bungalow and shove the old letters into William's hand. For a while he just frowns, trying to figure out what he's reading. Then smack bang he realises they're from someone who he used to know but who disappeared a long time ago. He leans back on a filing cabinet.

'What did he tell you?' William says to me, even though he's still looking at the letters.

'He didn't tell me anything. He ran away.' I rip into him about all the times Dad hit Mum because inside he was still a little boy whose father had left him in the middle of the night. That dad bottled it up and let it out on the people who cared about him most.

'You hurt my dad, and then my dad hurt us. And the only person who was always beautiful is gone.'

Thought I'd feel stronger by setting him straight but I don't feel right at all. My gut is all twisted up inside. William looks at me like I'm a hundred feet tall and my shadow would turn him to dust if he fell under it. He's got no words and even if he did there's nothing that can change what's done and dusted. Adults always think they know how teenagers feel 'cause they had once been the same age and 'have the benefit of hindsight', but he was never me. William's a stranger and it's too late for anything else. Now he's just fiddling with that gold cross on his necklace. Back and forth between his thumb and forefinger. One day he's gonna rub it into nothing. I look at my reflection in his eyes and realise they're full of tears.

'I need to have a lie down,' he says, stepping out of the shed. His foot lands heavy on the grass, knee takes the weight and for a second I think its going to buckle. But then he straightens himself out and walks to the house. Doesn't turn around once.

I'm not sure where to be now, so I sit in the bungalow for a good little while longer. The breeze skips in to inquire about the situation, wants to stir things up a bit. It ruffles through the papers. 'Catch me,' it says, but I'm not in the mood. I close the door before any of the papers fly off but by then the wind has gone looking for someone else to play with.

William didn't come back.

That night I'm the one scraping my fork around the plate because something has changed. We're eating spag bol and William's got a bit of sauce on his chin but I don't tell him. I think he's stifling a dragon roar and I don't want him to burn my face off. Maybe we'd be like a TV family that just sits in silence and lets the heat of harsh words slowly evaporate like steam from a boiled kettle.

'Good girl,' he says when I finish and put my cutlery together on the plate, tilted to the right like they do in fancy restaurants. No reason not to be polite even if I am being held against my will.

The phone rings suddenly and William clears his throat to get up. After a minute I know who it is and all my anger for Pat comes back clear as day.

'He's back home,' says William holding out the phone. I'm still feeling raw like I've fallen off my bike and have gravel rash inside my heart. But William just looks at me with his eyebrows up. So I take the phone and turn towards the wall because what I have to say is private.

'Dylan?'

'That's my name, don't wear it out.'

'Hey kiddo, how are you?'

'I'm not a kid.'

Pat pauses and even though I'm a million miles away

I know he's staring at his shoes 'cause he doesn't want to look me in the eye.

'No you're not. I know that. I just…'

I'm waiting for him to say he's made a mistake and is coming back to get me as soon as he can fill up the tank and have a cheeky Chiko roll before he hits the road.

'It might take a while but I think you're really gonna love living with your grandad. He's a good man, Dylan.'

'And what are you?'

Pat doesn't say anything so I pick up a pair of scissors from the side table and cut the cord in half. Maybe it wasn't the best reaction but if there's an investigation I'll say it was a crime of passion. I try to tie the ends of the phone cord into a sailor's knot but it doesn't work.

William comes back in with those uppity eyebrows again. 'Finished?'

He looks down and then his eyebrows follow. They turn into a frown. 'What in God's name happened here?' Now he's looking at my un-sailored knot. 'You can't just tie it back together!'

'Nothing here fits! Everything is the wrong size for my identity!'

'I don't know what that means, but you just can't… This is not acceptable!'

Well sure, none of it is. I especially did not accept Pat dumping me here or William shouting at me, so I shouted back.

'Aaaaaaahhhh!'

He doesn't say anything, just stares at me with goggle eyes. Then I remember he's a little bit deaf so I shout even louder.

'AAAAAAAHHHHHH!'

'THAT'S ENOUGH!'

'It's your fault the badness damaged my DNA. You gave it to my dad and he gave it to me!'

Apparently that *was* enough because I left William standing there like a stunned mullet, ran into the bedroom and slammed the door behind me. I watch as a dust ball whooshes into the air and falls gently back down into the corner. Inside the wardrobe I listen to William walking back and forth outside the door, creaking on the floorboards. I reckon that soon enough I'll know the sound of every board in the entire house. I could be blind and still make my way around.

When it goes quiet I push the door open. There's no one but that lazy wind outside, batting a tree branch against the window. *Slap*, *slap*. I creep out and sit in the middle of the floor. My head is spinning in a déjà vu. That's not a French chicken dish; it's life repeating. A word, a place, a feeling. My mama, my dad, William, Pat, Aunty Cecilia all running through my blood like drops of dye in water. Mixing into one another to make a new colour. Is it a pretty shade or still too dark for anyone to see what I am underneath?

24

Reckoning

William's got his days mixed up. Church is only open on a Sunday so he's three days early. But after breakfast he says, 'Will you come with me?' Which was not really a question since he was already holding the flyscreen door open that leads directly to the carport. So I sit in the front seat, which at least doesn't have spongy parts sticking out like the seats in Pat's bomb. I look at his long, bony fingers wrapped around the steering wheel like a skeleton. He's got the classical station on (yawn) and he's humming away, fingers dancing through the air like he's swatting flies. Men without rhythm shouldn't sing. Or drive and conduct at the same time.

I sigh loudly but it does no good. '*Ba bum bada bum bum bum*!' God help me! (That is a saying, not a call out to someone who probably does not exist.)

Even though I'm a heathen, being inside the church is a relief 'cause William finally puts a lid on it. You're only supposed to speak after the priest finishes his talk and then you say 'Amen', which is like a full stop. I didn't say Amen at Mum's funeral. I thought that would be lying, like a vegetarian who eats pork chops on the weekend. This church is empty apart from a woman cleaning the windows up the back. Margie used to say that men turned to God or the bottle to dissolve their sins. She said the Bible was only written for and by men who had screwed up and wanted another chance. She also used to say that Jesus was actually a 'swarthy lookin' fella', so I don't know how he ended up looking bleached like old curtains hanging in the sunroom.

Maybe William had brought me here to ask forgiveness. But then I realised the wardrobe in the corner wasn't open for business.

'I'm not getting baptised, and you can't make me,' I say. If that's his game he needs to know straight out who he's dealing with. The back door suddenly creaks open and all these people come in. Apparently it's church choir rehearsal. William says he can't sing to save himself but that listening is a joy. They have a proper conductor. Not like Mr Bony Fingers here. The songs are in a dead language, which means that people don't speak it anymore except in front of God 'cause he still remembers it.

If I ever had a baby I would name him or her Latin. It's the most beautiful thing I've ever heard.

Ave verum corpus, natum
de Maria Virgine,
vere passum, immolatum
in cruce pro homine.

This music is another kind of magic altogether. That's why people keep coming back every Sunday: to let the wounds that brought them there be healed.

I look at all the faces in the choir. What a bunch. There's a redhead teenage boy with braces and bad skin, a moustache man covered in tattoos, twin old ladies in wheelchairs and a bald woman with a dent in the side of her head. I guess you don't need sight to sing, because there is even a blind lady whose dog sits at her feet and looks bored the whole way through.

I wanted to hate William, I really did. Spent a lot of time on it over the years. If one single person could be the whole reason why you got hurt and lost people and felt wrong about yourself, then maybe the world would make a little more sense. But it isn't simple like that. And in the end it doesn't take the pain away. I don't want to be here, but I am also scared that one day I might wake up and find William gone. How can you explain that?

I looked at the faces in the choir. A few of them might have done bad things, been in jail even. But they could also make something beautiful together. William said very few of us are born with a halo or a red tail. We are all dancing up and down that ladder between heaven and hell. And then I know that William *has* come here to confess. Not to the man upstairs, but to me.

'I lost connection. With myself, my God and most of all my family. I left when my kids needed me the most, and I'm ashamed about that,' says William.

I tell William that Mama is connected to the land because everything of her, the bones, hair, teeth, even the last meal she ate, went into the ground.

He reaches out to touch my face, and I let him. We watch as the sun streams through the coloured windows and onto the pews. It's times like this I want to believe in God, that he could talk to me through the light. That divine intervention was a real thing and I could be born again with a few drops of holy water.

'I couldn't do it, look after them on my own. Lot of guilt with that kind of…failing,' William says with gravel in his voice.

How can the past be real if memories shift and change? I don't know what made my dad the way he was. Maybe he had darkness in his mind, weighing him down heavy like stones. Maybe William broke his heart by leaving. Or maybe it was something else altogether.

'Your dad, he didn't belong to anywhere or anyone. He said it was my fault, and maybe he's right about that.'

William's words bounce around the room and make a pattern. Lines travelling through him and along my arms. Reaching up and over the ceiling.

'But I want you to have a place. I want us to belong to each other.' His hands reach out and take mine. They don't feel as bony as they look. His skin is soft but those lines and patterns follow us out of the church and I'm worried it's all going to turn into a terrible mess of regrets and wishes pulling us down to a place we do not want to go. Words are cheap. That's what Margie used to say.

As soon as we get to the car William lights a cigarette. He leans against the bonnet and takes a long drag, trying to get as much smoke into his lungs as he can.

'That stuff will kill you,' I say.

He turns his head to the side and blows the smoke out, away from my face. 'Damn straight.'

Back home I think it might be okay to put some of my dresses in the wardrobe. Delicate things can't stay in a suitcase forever.

William sticks his head in through the open window. He's been in the bungalow the whole day, but I don't want to go back in there. I ruined it last time.

He's got something for me. It's a photo of Mum before I was born. She looks like a big little girl, smile so wide it could run off her face and skip down the street. And my dad is hugging her tight, their cheeks squished together. Next to them is William when his hair was twenty-three per cent less white than it is now. He's standing just a bit to the side with his mouth wide open like someone told a joke just before the camera clicked and he's thinking, 'Geez, that was a good one!' Now I'm smiling cause every inch of that photo is happy.

A billow of smoke whooshes into my room. It smells good. Someone's cooking snags.

When everything is new the days are long. Time yawns and every hour slides gently into the next. After bangers and corn chargrilled on the barbeque, sleep crawls into William's eyes. I tell him about the potato-rolling competitions back in Beyen and how kipflers are my least favourite for mash because it takes ages to peel the skins. He doesn't want to talk anymore which is fine by me 'cause I've got other things to explain. Like water. How it makes life but can take it away too. All the animals that live in it, feed from it, all the people who are taken by the floods, storms and tsunamis when the water rises up, crashes down, rushes in and rages out. Or does not come at all for a very long time so there are cracks in the thirsty ground. Circles and cycles keep life going and we are cocooned inside whether we like it or not.

William's got his eyes closed and says nothing. My heart sinks thinking all that knowledge has fallen on deaf ears. But then he nods his head.

'You're a good storyteller, my little channa.'

I don't know what that is, but I've never been anyone's channa before so I'll take it as a compliment. With too much whisky.

I share a lot of stories with William over the next few days. Sometimes we are quiet together and that is all right too. When we are shelling peas for Friday night fritters, all you can hear is *pop pop pop*! Little peas tumbling into the bowl just like Mum and me used to do, and that was nice, finding a memory in something small and green. One night as I'm going to bed I tell William that I've got his eagle, and I hold out the drawing he did all those years ago for my dad. Feels wrong to keep it hidden at the bottom of my backpack.

William's eyes are scanning it, and for a moment I think I've upset him again.

'It's not dirt,' I say quietly, pointing at the smudges of Vegemite that still hold Dad's fingerprints.

William squints closely, shaking the paper a little as recollection hits. 'It was Marmite,' he says. 'Almost the same but a little sweeter. That's what they had in Guyana when the Brits took over. Marmite, jaffa cakes and marching bands that played "God Save the Queen", except on May 26th when they celebrated not having to sing that song at all.

'That's not an eagle. It's a hoatzin. It's got an unusual gut that makes food in its belly smell like sauerkraut, so it's also called a stink-bird.'

It feels good to have made him happy.

'How we goin'? he asks.

'We goin' all right.'

He nods and turns off the bedroom light, takes the drawing with him.

I listen as the wooden floorboards creak with his steps down the hallway, until he falls into his own bed and dreams deep. Faraway from being and knowing, until the morning light taps him on the shoulder and brings him into the world again.

25

Joni

Every good story needs a disaster and a reckoning somewhere along the way, and you can be sure that's where we're heading. The whole journey is starting to make sense, to me at least. I've been brought to William to learn about the hoatzin bird. It will lead me to the sea where a shell will lead me to Joni, and Joni will lead me to the boat.

It's been two weeks since Pat left. I'm trying not to look back in anger because that can really damage your neck. Besides I've gritted my teeth long enough trying to really believe that 'gratitude is the only attitude'. The lady down the street in Beyen with big boobs and a liking for tight skivvies had that sticker on the back of her Datsun 180B. As well as 'Magic Happens'. I gave her the thumbs up whenever she drove by.

Maybe you have someone in your world so special you

can't imagine life without them. Well, that wasn't the case with me and my cousin Joni. When he came to visit he always brought that raggedy soft toy called Augie Belle. It had been Jules's when she was little. Maybe he hadn't been washed since then 'cause it looked like a grubby grey rat. But that Joni boy held onto Augie Belle, rubbed its droopy ear over his own making that little lobe boing back and forth like a cat flap. He would ogle at me without blinking, not even once.

What did Aunty Cecilia think I was going to do with *him*? He was way too short and quiet to play with. Cecilia said that Joni didn't talk at all. He understood everything but just chose not to use his words yet. William said that people grew into themselves at different speeds. In a way I grew used to having Joni around, like a wart on your thumb. It's annoying and shouldn't be there but isn't really doing you any harm. Especially since most of the time Joni just sat under the kitchen table like a pet dog that never barked.

My new food here is schnitzel. William got the idea from Father Ewald who taught him at school and said v instead of w. 'Vat is life vizout love?' Ewald was a priest, a man of the cloth. God's son knew about water. Turned it into wine and he could walk on top of it. Most of the other Fathers at William's school were flatliners: talked in a straight line with a voice that went nowhere. Others were harsh and cruel in their own ways, but

William didn't tell me about that. He said there were some things I didn't need to hear.

But Father Ewald was different. Even though he was devoted to doing God's work on Earth he was a restless soul. A wanderer searching for solace. Father Ewald was returned to his maker a long time ago but William still remembers the silly things he used to say. Like how his wallet was lined with onionskin because every time he looked inside it made him cry. William chuckled like it was hands-down the funniest thing he'd ever heard.

Apart from eating schnitzels we spent those first two weeks getting through the paperwork backlog in the shed. 'Fake it 'til you make it' is another bumper sticker that I kept telling myself to believe 'cause my guts still hurt, worrying that William would always feel like a relative stranger.

Even though Pat is in my bad books on every single page he feels more like home than ever. I'm not ready to say this out loud so I keep hanging up when he calls. Geez, he is persistent though, like one of those slow blowies on the windowsill that refuses to die no matter how hard you whack it with a tea towel. William had to buy a new phone after the scissor incident and I am sorry about that. But the new one has an in-built answering machine that blinks with a red light every time someone leaves a message:

'Yeah, hi Dylan, it's just—' Beep. Delete.

'So I'm just hoping to speak to—' Beep. Delete.

'G'day Dylan, look I know that—' Beep. Delete.

'William if you could please ask Dylan to—' Beep. Delete.

I pretty much just keep my finger down on that delete button for two whole weeks. The only other person to call is some Indian lady called Justine who wants to know if we can make a donation to save the children. I say I can donate all of my Timmy's fish logs but that isn't what they are looking for.

Deep down I know something bad is lurking around the corner. You can't hide from the darkness, no matter how nice and smiley you pretend to be. I hold a workshop with myself to figure out if I can still escape this family exchange program. How could Pat just dump and run when he knew all about the troubles with my dad? He should have found another way. Mum said that sometimes you can't see the smoke signals until it's too late. Like her and Dad. If he hadn't disappeared we would've run away for sure. Sometimes when it all got too much I rocked back and forth, telling myself to stay solid on the inside not soft like a machine.

William always watches from a distance, not knowing how I feel and maybe thinking I'm a robot, not human at all.

But one night everything changes. I'd left the window open to catch a cool breeze and that's when I hear that hoatzin bird calling me. I climb out the window and run. Pieces of gravel get stuck between my toes but I keep hobbling down that road with the hoatzin soaring above. Cut through the bush and take the trail between the trees where the night owls keep watch. 'Stay close, follow fast,' they tell me.

Again I wonder if the owls know where I'm going—do birds have the same, shared mother tongue? I follow those wings flying high above, but then my toes curl round the edge of a cliff. If this is a dream I want to take myself out of it right now. I look down and see my feet, bloodied and bruised. Throbbing.

The hoatzin is calling.

'What do you want to show me? Help me home!' I run, half-fall, trip and over the side for real! Down the slope and onto the beach. The hoatzin squawks at me: 'Into the cave, into the cave!'

It's most certainly a trap but he will not bring me home until I do it. Fists in front of me like a fighter waiting for a sneaky left hook, I walk further down until I can't see fingers in front of my face. Might be travelling to Middle Earth for all I know, until I turn the corner and blinding light shines into my eyes. There it stands, the biggest seashell you have ever seen, curling round and round and up to the cave ceiling. The inside of the shell glows like a thousand light bulbs. There's an invisible thread tied around my waist pulling me towards it and I try to step back but my feet push me closer still. It is wondrous but I'm frightened all the same. I climb up towards the top and all the while I can hear the sea outside, so loud I'm almost deafened. I hear waves crash onto the shore then splinter into a million pieces. And inside all that crashing, they are whispering, because they do not want me to know their secrets.

Then I hear her voice: *'Reviens à moi!'* Mum is at the very top of the shell. I cling onto the sides as I climb higher. Now it's raining rusty fish. They prick and scratch my skin with their cold brown scales. I close my eyes as light pours over me, from yellow to white to bright beyond bright. Higher, go higher, take me sky high back to *Maman...*

I feel sick, seasick, the room spins and I want to get off. Turn my head to the side and here it all comes, burns my throat on the way up and onto the floor. I stumble out of my bedroom and out into the garden where the rain pelts down, hitting me hard like liquid bullets. It says, 'Stupid girl, feel how stupid you are!'

I start digging in the ground: if I cannot have her spirit then I will find her body. And it doesn't matter that she went into the ground at Beyen, that dull and throbbing pain is bringing her here, dragging her bones beneath the earth, sliding her body through the mud, worms, roots and all. My nails are black with dirt as my hands dig fast and frantic. I am gone to it all and soon there are thirteen holes across the garden seeking and searching for Mama. *Maman, aide-moi, reviens à moi. Où es-tu?* But I have tricked myself again, and the rain pelts my skin harder to punish me for thinking I can bring her back through dreams or real life.

My head is thumping when William comes racing out. He tries to lift me off the ground but I am as limp as a ragdoll with nothing left inside.

'Come on, come now!' He crouches on the ground. Wraps his arms around me, holds tight. We are rocking back and forth because he knows it's the only thing he can do.

'Am I a real girl?'

'Come on, my baby.'

'Am I still real?'

'You're here with me.'

But that's not an answer.

Next thing I'm back in bed. Dry and warm. Poor William is on his hands and knees cleaning up the sick. No words, just wiping it all away.

And then his cool hands are on my forehead feeling for a fever. 'You feel bad? Got some nasty belly work there?'

'That sea is sick. It's making rusted fish.'

William's got his worried eyes on nodding to me with all the understanding that he can muster. He tells me that I'm safe now and the best place to be is bed. Cecilia is coming in the morning with Jules and Joni, but if I'm not up to it they can stop by later. I hope later turns into never because I'm in a bad way and want to have my tongue taken out so I don't have to speak to anyone ever again.

William goes and then I'm alone, but I keep my eyes open—I don't want to go back where I was. Feel the bottom of my feet and they're smooth but something has punctured my chest all the same.

The rain falls gently again on the window, but I turn the other way. Sea, rain, river or tap. Water is poison to me now.

In the morning my stomach calls out for something so I shuffle into the kitchen. Before I can turn away Cecilia is out of her seat and squeezing me tight against her boobs.

'You coming down with something?'

'No, I'm staying up.'

She looks at William, confused.

'I don't want to hear about any more birds and I'm not ever dreaming again,' I say before heading back to bed. I take an apple on the way.

William nods and then everyone else does too.

Cecilia and Jules pop their heads in before they go and they tell Joni to say goodbye to his cousin. But he doesn't say anything. Just takes in a big breath of air and blows it out again with a long, heavy sigh. Like he is ninety-three years old and tired of it all.

I don't know how long I sleep but when I wake it is dark and my timing is all out of whack. I want to start the day but it's coming to an end. William is watching the cricket on TV. He stands up suddenly with a whoop and then sits down again.

'Yes sir!' he shouts at the TV.

I make myself a cherkin sandwich (cheese and gherkin) and sit down next to him.

'This is their last chance. Just plain sloppy.'

I don't know who is plain or sloppy, so I just nod.

'How are you feeling, Channa?'

'Hungry.'

'Well, that's a good sign.'

He reaches into his pocket and fumbles around.

'Joni left something for you.'

Now you won't believe this. Still hardly can myself. William pulls out a little curly seashell and puts it in the palm of my hand. Before I can say anything he's up on his feet, yelling at the TV with all his hoo-ha again.

'No doubt about that!! *Howzat! Howzat! Howzat!*'

26

Buttons

I stare at that shell all night. Hold it up to the moon-light and remember just how I'd climbed up to the very top heading towards Mum. A miracle, mystery and natural wonder of the world all in the palm of my hand. How did that little boy with no words know about my dream? How could he have seen where I'd been? The hoatzin had led me to Joni and now where would Joni lead me?

The next morning William has to look after Joni because each Tuesday both of his mums are bringing home the bacon. Joni's sitting at the table with a jar of buttons, drawing a picture. I sit at the table and pour milk on my Rice Bubbles.

'Thank you for my shell.'

Joni just keeps scribbling.

'How did you get into my dream?'

He cocks his head to the side but doesn't say anything. I crunch my cereal real loud and tap my foot hoping that my annoyances will trip him up. But he keeps on colouring. I want to tell him he needs to stay inside the lines but I manage to hold my tongue. Joni finishes the picture and pushes it in my direction. It's pretty bad, but there we are, looking like scarecrows holding each other's stick hands. I'm mostly green and he is pink and orange. We have no necks.

I go brush my teeth and when I come back he's sitting in my bedroom on the floor.

'Turn around,' I tell him. I get dressed while he faces the corner. I know he's scrunching his eyes shut but I still watch him on the off-chance he tries to take a peep.

I'm not really interested in having a one-sided conversation with a mute four-year-old, so I don't say anything. William knocks on the door and says he has a chess game with his friend Ruben. Some people say chess is a spectator sport, which is crazy. No one runs and there are too many rules about horses and prawns. William says Ruben was in Wodonga. They play over the phone which means he has to move his own prawns *and* Ruben's and Ruben has to do the same on the other end of the line. They'll be at it forever, but old people don't care about time because their brains go round and round in circles. William puts on a cartoon about pink fairies chasing elves and says that after the game we'll all go for a walk and get fish and chips for lunch.

Well, I'm fourteen, for goodness sake! William's too busy moving Ruben's knight down to his queen to notice that I'm going for a walk to buy something anyways. Pat gave me the very last of his boot money, pulled out a crumpled ten-dollar note from his stinky right sock on the night before he left. I wasn't going to keep it. I wasn't going to keep anything from Pat.

Halfway to the shops, who turns up but Mr Mute. He's hiding behind trees every time I turn around, thinking I can't see him except his jar of buttons is jiggling like a full packet of smarties. I tell him to bugger off home, but he just holds his breath like that's gonna make him invisible or something.

In the end I tell him to come walk next to me 'cause I don't like being stalked. Having some company is okay for a while, but then I realise we're just ambling about and I'm lost. I don't want to frighten Joni because I'm the bigger person and supposed to know what's what. So I sit on a tree that's fallen over, scared of being so tall.

'I'm just gonna…have a rest.'

But I'm not foolin' this kid. Joni shoves his pudgy little hand inside his button jar and takes out a shiny turtle-green shell. He hands it to me like this is some sort of currency exchange except I don't know what

I'm supposed to give him in return. The only thing I have that he does not, is words. So I think about what is worth a green turtle-shell button. Even though I'm not having anything to do with water anymore, the facts about it are solid and interesting. My *rancorous and discordant history* with the substance should not stop Joni from being educated.

'Pure water has no smell or taste. It also has a pH level around 7,' I say.

A frown floats across Joni's face but then he nods like he's chewed on this fun fact and decided it tastes all right. I know this because he digs around in his jar and gives me another button, all bubbled and brown.

Soon I've forgotten we are lost and in potential danger of being kidnapped or falling into a wormhole and ending up back in 1956. This is how it goes:

Blue pearl: breathing in and out every day uses up more than half a litre of water.

White swirl: A jellyfish and a cucumber are both ninety-five per cent water.

Grass green: sound travels five times faster underwater.

Purple and pink dots: Camels can drink ninety-four litres of water in about three minutes.

Big fat orange: koalas are one of only two animals that do not need to drink water. They get it from gum leaves. I do not know the other one.

Another turtle-shell: Blood plasma is fifty per cent water.

Red ridges: It takes forty-one kilograms of water to make one slice of bread.

After the red-ridge button I go a bit fuzzy and can't think of anymore important water facts that end in a full stop. So we stand up and walk along the sleeping tree. I jump off at the end and Joni hops onto my back. I carry him all the way and only stop when he needs to do a wee. I feel it, not because he pees on my back, but because there is something strange going on between us, like the synchronicity me and Pat had when we were on the road. Joni is in my mind and I am in his. We are a little bit psychic and that is the only way you can talk to someone who doesn't speak.

We sit on a bench out front of the fish and chip shop with our battered flake and potato cakes like it has always been this way. Can taste salt in the air, straight off the back of a wave. Surely that can't do me any harm. Joni is still small enough to swing his legs under the bench. Walking home again I jump onto the sleeping tree and hold my hand out to Joni but he just walks alongside on the ground. When I get to the end, Joni holds his hand out for *me*.

'Checkmate!'

I don't know what Ruben needed to check but

William was laughing from his belly. 'Never see it coming, good sir. I'll go easy next time.' He hangs up and sees us staring at him, then a look of horror spreads across his face.

'Good Lord, what on earth's happened?'

William thinks the tomato sauce on Joni's cheek is smeared blood. I tell him where we've been and what we did, and I might as well have said we'd gone to the moon and back.

First I think he's mad 'cause I absconded with Joni, then a smile cuts across his dial like I'd suddenly sprung out of a wheelchair and run the City to Surf.

'It was just to the shops. I'm a teenager. That's the only place we can really go.'

But then William got upset. 'Dylan, you have to tell me if you're gonna go somewhere. Things can happen when you're by yourself.'

But we were together is what I want to say. I reckon he was mad at himself for not knowing we'd been gone on his watch.

'Joni wandered off a couple of months ago. You can't look after him by yourself.'

He thinks I am a retard just like those Beyen BMX boys with jeering weasel smiles, calling me Abo Spazzo. Joke was on them 'cause I'm neither. When you become an adult everything makes you sad, mad or scared. Truth be told, I think William is one and three. Sad that

I've come to him so far down the track and scared he'll lose me all over again, and maybe Joni too.

I put my cat-bum lips on, take Joni's hand and storm off into my bedroom. Joni is the only one young enough to just let me be. We sit and draw together under my desk. I'm not drawing anything except my emotions and that is just a circle of red and purple that goes round and round until it looks like a black hole ready to swallow me up if I stare in too deep.

I sigh louder than I mean to. Joni takes a big breath in and sighs too. He is me and I am him. And from now on that's the way it is. He has two mums, I have none. I had a volcanic dad, he has an uncle-pa. We are ying and yang, Cheech and Chong, up and down, right and wrong. We'll always be together unless a certain someone tries to stickybeak his way back in.

'Yeah, Dylan, look I know that—' Beep. Delete.

'Dylan, it's been a month now and—' Beep. Delete.

'Okay, well, I'm gonna leave it to you. I just want to—' Beep. Delete.

When he sees me all weighed down with sorrow William takes me to proper church on a Sunday and that is not a bad thing because I can wear a pretty dress if I want to. When I only want to be casually religious I wear trackie dacks and thongs. They are pink so it's still respectful. I'm not going in the box though. Makes me think about Mum's funeral and me looking for a way out. William says I don't have to go up and get the biscuit and drink because I'm not baptised. He goes up though, every time. I ask if it's all right to be black and Catholic and William says religion, race and spirituality are all different things. He says it doesn't have anything to do with colour. It's about faith and belonging. But I've never heard of someone having Christmas and Hanukah, which is what we celebrated for Lally the Jewish girl at after-school care back in Beyen. William says people are often contradicting themselves and they could be richer for that. Like a proper church choir made up of criminals and the ninety-year-old wheelchair twins Astrid and Agatha who all sound like angels.

The church is a funny place. William says it has hurt a lot of people in many ways including himself, but that is also not for me to know about. Not right now.

That night Joni stays over because Aunty Cecilia and Jules are going out. Jules plays guitar in a band called Halcyon Daze and they have a concert at the pub. Aunty Cecilia just watches because she doesn't have a musical bone in her body. I tapped her joints with my special fork once and they all sounded flat.

Joni sleeps on the floor of my room, but in the early morning hours he creeps into my bed and strokes my face. His breath is sweet like condensed milk straight from the can. I can see my reflection in his glassy brown eyes and for a moment, I think I *am* here. I am.

I close my eyes and drift away with his warm breath on my face. But when I wake up Joni is gone. Shadows creep across the room like a daddy-long-legs spider. Even though it's early morning, the moon has not yet gone to sleep. Its blue light guides me out, down the hallway. I stop at William's door. He's still asleep with a splutter and a snore.

Out the back through the laundry, tiptoing down the garden path. And that's when I see them. Buttons on the ground, all laid out like coloured breadcrumbs.

A path for me. Joni is playing hide and seek. Now I'm not sure if this is another dream but I dare not turn back. I must find him before William wakes because things can happen, yes, that's true. Children can vanish into the bush forever. So now I panic, picking up those buttons and shoving them in my pyjama pocket just to feel closer to him. I trip over a stubborn tree root, fall flat on my face. Will I see a silhouette of that hoatzin flying past the moon? Has he got into Joni's little head and led him out here? 'Keep your hands off him,' I say. He's not for you! Orange button, then lilac, rose, ash, cobalt.

Getting wet, cold mud, slipping down like quick-sand. Heart races—he's up ahead.

Down in the muddy banks of the mangroves, Joni taps the side of the boat with his finger. It's wood. Not metal. Someone's had their fun and now it's stranded, too far into the mangroves to move. Joni doesn't care. I swear he's talking to himself, like when little kids think no one's watching. Secret worlds. But then he knows I'm here. Nods at the rowboat then looks straight at me as if to say, 'This what you been looking for?'

And now I know there's another answer. When sleeping and waking worlds collide, your dreams let you escape. The boat! Wild mangrove branches wrapped around it so tight they're part of it: planks of wood returning to tree.

I crouch down by the side and slide my hand over the branches and along the rim until a splinter pierces my finger. The boat wants to take me out on the water, to beckon Mum's spirit into being. For real this time. Besides, rowboats aren't meant to stay still. They must row, sway, float, carry treasures from the sea or steal time away so men can sit for hours waiting for their catch. There are a couple of old beer bottles under the seat and I see a crab scuttle away when I step inside. A handful of Joni's buttons are scattered on the floor like rose petals at a wedding. He's been here before.

This is where Joni went that time he disappeared. He studies that old collection of buttons in the boat, colours faded from many days in the sun. Curls his finger round a wisp of his brown golden hair and hums to himself.

I'm looking far off down the channel and out to the open sea. *Maman, aide-moi, reviens à moi. Où es-tu?*

Is the water still playing tricks, or will it deliver us home? I feel the sadness sweep along those bony branches still clinging to the boat. But they know it's time to let go. A new journey is coming.

27

Our secret caper

I don't tell William about that morning later when the dawn breaks and everything clears away. He would have a heart attack, 'cause he's always saying kids and water do not mix. We are quiet as can be sneaking back inside the house. Didn't matter, William was still snoring in the exact same position.

I make Joni Coco Pops because they are for special occasions and we are celebrating, even though no one else knows why.

I need a scheme. I sit and write with Joni's coloured pencils. Stick it in an envelope from William's writing desk to make it more professional and run to the letterbox out front. Sometimes you have to lose something to get back what you love, and I don't even think about William getting hurt all over again.

When Aunty Cecilia comes to get Joni, I've already read it in my head a thousand times but I pretend it's all a big surprise when she brings it in and smiles know-ingly at me.

'Baboo, you got a letter!'

'For goodness sake, if that's the gas company again...'

She hands it to William who frowns when he doesn't recognise the handwriting. Fumbles with the envelope and now everyone's looking at him.

> To whom it may concern,
>
> Joni would like to go to the fish and chip shop every Tuesday when William plays his phone chess with Ruben. He asked me to accompany him so I can place the order, eat at the kiosk and walk back home with him. He does not have a Tuesday treat at the moment and is bored of watching the fairy video. I am very safe with roads and know how to poke dangerous strangers in the eyes with two fingers. And anyway they mostly have bad teeth so I will look out for rotten smiles.
>
> Yours in good faith,
> Dylan Freeman.

I rub my eyes because all this asking, waiting and worrying is making me feel tired.

'You know that path well, eh?' says Aunty Cecilia.

I nod and say you can see my footprints in the ground I've gone up and down so often. And William's smiling at the letter but having a conversation with himself in his head.

'It's just that Joni's only little and...'

Here we go. It's always *just that* something. It's never just yes-what-a-top-idea-good-on-you-for-suggesting-it-in-the-first-place.

But then Aunty Cecilia says how lovely it is that I want to have some quality time with Joni. That I'm like his deedee—his big sister.

William nods like he's agreed all along. My heart is racing because I can't believe I've got away with it. And if there is a heaven I hope God still lets me in because it was only a half-lie. I *will* be spending extra top-quality time with Joni even if the fish and chip shop is a red herring. Maybe a John Dory as well.

Finally next Tuesday rolls around and Operation Rowboat is about to begin. An 'Operation' like the police storming Terry Brankett's house for illegal green plants or that woman down on Hanerking Crescent who sold all her dead husband's leftover cancer pills to people who weren't even sick.

William clears his throat and flicks through his wallet, gives me a $10-note and says, 'Only juice, nothing fizzy.' Little does he know the night before I made us Vegemite sandwiches and a little snaplock bag of barbecue shapes (which Woolworths finally has in stock). Not so many that he might suspect something, but just enough to take the edge off when we need more fuel. He straps a watch onto my wrist. 'It's a digital, yeah?' he says. Like I should be glad it wasn't the old-style time that I learnt in grade three. *Mon Dieu*! He gives us fifteen minutes to walk there, half an hour to eat and fifteen to come back. I'll have to work quick, but with Joni by my side anything is possible.

We do go down to the shops but straight past Ye Olde Fish & Chippery and into Mitre 10 where I buy a sample tin of green paint that was half-price 'cause they're not selling that colour anymore. The man goes into the storeroom and comes back with some old paintbrushes he says we can have. For free! Mum used to say one way or another everything had a price tag. But there are no strings attached here; I checked the bag twice before we left.

When we get to the mangroves I can't remember where to go and no matter which way we walk the boat is nowhere. Maybe it's been stolen. Or taken by someone who actually owned it. Maybe this is all over before it's begun. I get real hot, can feel my heart booming through my rib cage. It isn't just the boat. It's the idea that I might have to stay with William forever and that is a very long time to be with anyone who is stranger kin. Besides, where will Mum go if I can't get her to Paris?

I feel hot tears slipping down my cheeks.

'And now?' Joni says with his eyes, lost like a dog waiting outside a supermarket sure his owner is never coming back.

I just shake my head because I have no idea. Joni walks back the way we've come. And I'm glad to be following. He knows that if we just go a little further down the first path we will see the bend before the river, before the fallen tree before the boat.

And here we are.

I tell Joni he is my child labourer, that this is a special job only small and nimble hands can complete. First we have to pull the gnarly branches off the boat. They're all twisted in and around it, holding on for dear life. It's dead weight and gotta go.

Joni's pretty useless. He collects all the branches I pull off and puts them in a pile. Like we're gonna build a campfire later or something. And then I have to push the boat as far as I can out of the wet mud. Joni just points in the direction I should be pushing and shakes his head when I fall over and get my knees and hands all dirty.

I glare at him. 'Pull your weight,' I want to say.

And then we paint in silence. All you can hear is the tap of a brush on the rim of the paint tin and the swish of bristles on wood. It's like meditation. Stroke right, left, right, left again. Lets your mind wander any which way it pleases. *Parfait.*

．

The next Tuesday I wake up with a hard gut. A knot of worry strangling excited butterflies that make me feel so full the only thing I eat for breakfast are the leftover Rice Bubbles from the bottom of Joni's bowl. I'm worried the boat will be gone and excited it might still be there. It isn't mine and maybe that would be a strike against me with the man upstairs, but that is a chance I am willing to take. I walk extra fast because I wanna know one way or another. Phew. I breathe a big sigh of relief when we round the corner. I see Joni's pile of campfire branches first and then the boat, just as we'd left it. I don't need to tell Joni what to do. He hands me a paintbrush and gets going.

I smile. This kid's all right.

As soon as one Tuesday comes and goes I am counting down to the next. Joni is too. Sometimes it's lonely being small and even though he doesn't know what the secret is all about he understands we are sharing something. Knowing that makes him feel a little bigger. I heard on *Oprah* that you have to visualise your dreams if you want them to 'arrive in your reality'. Even though she was on TV, Oprah looked straight at me when she said that. Like she knew where I was going and that painting a boat pea green with your mute cousin was a good place to start. I will send Oprah a postcard from Paris once we get there. I think she'd like that.

People say that the best time of day is in the morning before the world has really woken up and I have to agree. I am glad William has given me the digital watch because I can set it to 5 am every Tuesday morning and make our sandwiches fresh. One time I made us banana and peanut butter and then another time grated carrot and cream cheese but we did not like that. It tasted too raw. Once I even took some chicken drumsticks left over from dinner the night before. William worried he was getting geriatric, thinking food was there when it wasn't.

'Sometimes I have a snack at night,' I said, just to throw him off.

We've been lucky with the weather, real lucky. Hot but not harsh with a breeze to take the edge off while we paint. I can hum Joni's little melody off by heart now. And once in a while I catch him whispering to Augie Belle like he is keeping him up to date on our progress.

On our lunchbreaks we throw the crusts into the trees because our hair is already curly. We sit with our feet over the edge of the boat, looking at the speckled sun that peeks through the mangrove branches. Hear the waves tumble in and out with the tide, far down out of sight. Augie Belle propped up on the tip of the boat keeping watch for us.

Once when we were coming back I found a really long brown and white feather stuck in a tree branch. I wondered if the hoatzin was leaving his own trail for me to find. Then again, I'm no ornithologist. Even though I did know there was a James Bond born in 1900 who knew all about birds from the Caribbean, and that the spy man in the movies was named after him. I learnt that from *Sale of the Century*. I wonder if the hoatzin is on strike, because I haven't seen him in my dreams for a long time. He helped bring me to the boat and I should've listened to what else he had to say. Maybe he figures I'm not black enough to know all the stories that lie under my skin.

I still fear someone will come and collect what's theirs. It definitely could happen 'cause as I said before surprises are mostly not nice. And what about Mum— now I'd found the boat (or at least *a* boat), where was she? I don't know enough to understand what the spirit world is like. Maybe there's a lot of traffic or paperwork so you can't always be with your loved ones on Earth. But a sign would be nice.

Couple of days later Pat sends me a photo of Mum's gravestone. Got a good deal on the granite from Dave, the letter says, but I don't think talking about money and dead people is right. The engraving says: 'Juliet Lanfore. A wonderful mother to Dylan.' I stare at my name for the longest time. Some person must have sat in a workshop and carved it into that stone. You can't rub carvings out so my name will keep me there forever with Mum's name in a long row of other headstones. Where are all those dead people now? Are they all going back to their fatherlands and motherlands across the sea?

'I'm your real girl,' I tell Joni and he nods that little head of his for so long I have to tell him to stop.

But one week later a cloud floats into the sky and hovers over my head. For so long I'd waited for that blackness in William and Aunty Cecilia to spill out of them, maybe seep out from my own skin too. I'd been waiting for the next volcano to erupt, screaming and shouting and smashing of things that were precious and could not be replaced. But it hasn't come. Sure, William and Aunty Cecilia argued, teased, rubbed each other the wrong way, but it turns out their skin is just a colour, not a feeling. Not a bad one at least.

Now I am the one who feels bad, untruthful with them all especially Joni, 'cause he can't come with me when I leave.

I am doing the same cowardly thing Pat has done to me. Leave someone behind. But until I get in that boat and take Mum back I will feel half-finished and undone with no marrow in my bones or spine in my back. Can't stand straight like that.

28

The night sea with its black heart

Everything you're too scared to ask for ends up swirling around in your dreams. Then you see just how strong those invisible ties to other people are. That hoatzin bird finally returns one night, picks those ties up in his claws and tugs so hard I am lifted into the sky. Then I'm looking down at the ground, following his shadow as he flies over the earth. We travel so fast I can hardly breathe; the cold air hurts my lungs. But then I see the hand of Beyen welcoming me home once more. 'Come closer,' it beckons. Sit inside and feel the warm, hard metal against your back.

Everything feels strange and distant now. Those ties around my legs and arms are hurting so he lets me go. 'See for yourself,' he says. As I fall, the ground comes up towards me until everything goes black. The hoatzin's taken me inside Pat's memory bank. I see his hand sweep across a desk, sends his boss's papers flying into the air, before he storms out. I see Pat grab money from a kid busking on Watson Street, right out of his violin case. Just to feed those stupid machines 'cause his wallet is lined with onionskin. Not a single cent within. No fridge anymore, just an esky holding a sixpack of Coopers pale ale. His head pounds, thinking, 'What have I got left to sell? What can go?' Keeps drinking until the numbness takes hold. Before I can see anything else I'm wrenched up into the air by the hoatzin. I watch those ties leading back to Pat rip away from his ankles, arms and neck. They leave burn marks dark like red wine. He looks up at me.

'Wait!' we both cry, but I am travelling again through the night sky.

When I wake, my pillow is wet with tears. I've thought about the hoatzin enough for him to come back to me to see that I'm sorry for doubting him. But, oh, what sorrow! I've never heard Pat wail so loud, all alone and empty the way he was. Now the tears falling are mine because I cut those ties, deleted all his messages trying to tell me how sad he was. I run into William's room and my words are all covered in snot but I have to let him know.

'He's not safe, he's not safe!' is all I can say. I get William to phone Pat but a lady's voice says the number has been disconnected. DISCONNECTED! From what, to where? He needs a divine water intervention. I told William, but he didn't understand why Pat couldn't just turn on his own tap and pour himself a glass. People who are down and out don't know what they need. That's the whole point of intervening.

'We're here, and he's there.' William points to the map on the wall, demonstrating how inconvenient the whole situation is. Time and geography are not on our side, so William starts walking his own thoughts around the room, scratching his head. Makes a phone call and another, writes a name down and calls another number twice before someone called Sean picks up. A lot of shoulder shrugging and head shaking later, William says it's all happening. Sean's sister-in-law's brother is a taxi driver in Wilcott, which is the nearest town to Beyen. He'll drive over to Pat's house with four glasses and a bottle of water from the IGA on the corner of Bray and Kiness Street. He'll put those glasses down on the doorstep and fill them all with water while I pray the magic into each and every glass.

I squish my eyes so tightly I think they might pop out the back of my head. We're not home and hosed yet. What if Pat knocks the glasses over when he gets back from the pub, one too many beers in his belly and not enough sense in his head? Then all those ties that had let me see the state he was in would be severed for good. I wait that night, watch William's old videos of

Magnum PI and *Knightrider* that are in the cupboard under the TV. At 10.29 pm the phone rings. I roll myself out of the beanbag and run down the hallway. In my head I play a worse-case scenario: 'This is the police. Do you know a Pat O'Brien?'

But as soon as I pick up the phone I know it's him.

'Thought for a minute you'd come back.'

I reckon Pat could see my smile down the telephone line. He'd put those water glasses in each corner of the living room. Filled them to the top and drank the rest for good measure. My heart was beating fast when I told Pat what I'd seen. Him messing up Ray's office and stealing that busker boy's money just to play the pokies some more.

For the longest time there was silence and I thought the line must have gone dead.

'I'm...I tried to pay that kid back but his dad clobbered me one. Dylan, how can you know those things?'

I didn't have an answer Pat would understand so I told him I was tired and had to go to bed.

People can feel snow coming when their bones begin to ache, or they get headaches before a storm blows over. Something is stirring in me too 'cause my fingers have pins and needles. Feels like the nerves have been cut but can't stop tingling. No matter how many weather forecasts they make, sometimes it all changes and it's too late to battle down the hatches. A sunshower can turn into a windstorm or a rumbling cloud collides with another and lets loose with a furious downpour pelting the earth with golf-ball hailstones. The only difference between humans and nature is malice. That is cruelty and wickedness rolled up into a fancy word. Nature does what it does not to please or punish, just to be true to itself. Humans use words to be cruel and hands to hurt. Because we are fearful in a way that nature will never understand. And even if no one feels the stirring but me there is something coming that can not be stopped or changed.

But talk about timing. On the night of the pre-Christmas barbeque, for goodness sakes. Aunty Cecilia wanted to cancel because Micky Roberts the weather guy, whose shaggy hair makes him look like a dog with low brain power, said a storm front was sweeping across from the west, driving through winds at more than 100 kilometres an hour.

'What about all those sausages? I went bulk!' William was cranky that the meat might go off just because of a little breeze. 'Might not even happen. That Roberts guy doesn't look like he's firing on all cylinders,' he says, trying to convince Aunty Cecilia.

'Some of them are already on their way,' says Jules.

This party is almost entirely made up of Jules's family, who were flying in for Christmas. They all live somewhere else, not as far as Beyen but far enough to pack a bag and get on a plane.

None of this feels right. Having lots of people in a small space with meat, flies and wind is never a good idea. And okay sure, they're all related to Joni, but they'll only ever be strangers-in-law to me. I should say that at this point William had bought me a new dress from Target's summer range and it wasn't even on special. It is metallic blue with puffy shoulders, a dress like Tina would have worn on *Young Talent Time*. I did want to 'rock da frock', like William said I should.

I can smell those chicken sausages: gourmet they are, with some kind of spice to bring out the poultry even more. William has a silly hat on with a cup holder and straw attached so he can sip and turn the meat at the same time. Says it's important to replenish those fluids you lose while manning the barbeque. His apron has a fake beer gut made out of rubber. It looks funny because it's white and he is not, and besides he already has a genuine beer gut. But he is in his element.

Jules' grandma, Kathleen, introduces herself to me. She is nice and wrinkly, hair done like we used to do Margie's. She calls me darls and asks me to top up her champers on three different occasions. I have to refill from the bottom 'cause she hands me an empty glass every time. I show Joni how to put Cheezels on his fingers like edible rings but his mouth is so small he can only stuff half of one in at a time. The other half falls to the ground and someone's golden retriever called Cookie rushes over and gobbles it up.

But by 7 pm things start to get out of control. Jules's relatives just keep coming, like sheep in a line waiting to be clipped or dipped, except they are all coming to meet *me*. Tall, short, fat, thin, loud, quiet, red and freckly—the whole united nations of relatives that I did not know anything about. Edwin, Nina, Birgit, Michael, Gaz, Claire, Alex, Ade, Steve and Linda, Aunty Ali, Moni, Olivia, Dave, Nari, Jess, Jenna, Uncle Abe, who helped make Joni, Kez, Mez, Jenny, Dr Kath, Dan, Amina, Sofia, Marla, and Andy K for good measure. They all smile and shake my hand like I'm the queen hosting a garden party. Everyone asks me questions or tries to explain who's who and where they are from. It's all just a blur of noise to me. I feel like the odd one out and the even one in. How do you make sense of people on the same family tree as you but far, far down or somewhere on a branch way up on the left?

Turns out Micky Roberts was right about those winds. First sign is the napkins blowing around the place like giant cabbage moths, which Joni thinks is a funny game, jumping round the garden trying to step on them as they land. It's all getting a bit too loud for my eyes. Too much colour and motion, kids helping themselves to my bowl of Cheezels, adults laughing so hard they have to lean back and look at the sky. Ladies hooting with one another picking at their blouses with 'It's sheer but not *too* sheer,' and leaning in with quiet voices: 'No no, she said it was back on. Wouldn't touch him with a bargepole, but what do I know? Maybe the drongo's donger still works!'

And then the music changes when a big bloke calls out, 'Let someone with a bit of taste take over!' Quickly followed by, 'Is Tina all right for your refined sensibilities?'

I get all excited, but it wasn't my Tina, it was 'Simply the Best' Tina, which is okay but not when everyone sings so loud they're ahead of the song jumbling it all up. I need to get out of this shindig before the buzzing in my ears short-circuits my brain. I run over to William.

'How's my little channa? Do you want another sausage?'

I take two and sit inside under the kitchen table thinking how nice the party would have been if Mum and Pat were here too. Pat might've held out his hand and said, 'Let me spin you round, little lady!' I think about how I smashed my snow globe on the ground, watched the water trickle into the cracks. I feel so alone, and my eyes sting with tears. When my nose drips I have to wipe it on the sausage napkin.

Then there's a really loud BANG 'cause the tarpaulin outside has fallen over in the wind and is heading towards the back fence. I reach into my pocket and run my fingers over my metal fish, try to count the scales and calm myself down. I'm still here. Breathe.

The sky has turned black and the rain comes hammering down like a bag of stones on the roof. Squeals and shouts as everyone piles inside and from under the table all I see are dirty, muddy shoes.

'Oi! Leave your shoes at the door. Backtrack, please!' William calls out as people run inside.

I want to backtrack too, out of this place right now.

'Hello! Who's hiding down there?'

I feel shame burn my teary cheeks and run out before that stranger's voice can catch me—straight into the wardrobe. Four walls of solitude and all I do is listen to my breathing get longer and deeper.

William comes in and asks if I'm scared of the storm.

'There's so much noise! Too many people filling up my head!'

He goes into the kitchen and tells everyone to put a lid on it, but no one's listening. The wind feels like it's trying to get inside, banging on gates and slamming doors, prising back the roof one tile at a time and that rain does not stop. A lightning bolt slits open clouds that have been saving up their rain for years. *Crack!* Thunder booms and the power goes. Shrieks of excitement then worry as people try to find their way around.

'Dave, you got Nari?'

'Hey, Kez, watch the steps there. Go slow.'

Then I hear the rain say, 'Look kid, this is it. Go now or it may be too late.'

The house is creaking like it can't hold its weight anymore and I run without thinking, away from the shouting and screaming. A pole from the tarpaulin smashes through the kitchen window. Then there's nothing but panicked voices: 'Get down! Where is he? Come on, no leave it. I've got you!'

My feet are taking me to the only place I can think of. It's not ready. Half-painted and probably leaky, but I know it will move now, out into the channel and down to the sea. The rain is right; this could be my only chance so I have to be brave. I've forgotten my shoes and something spikes my foot. A sharp breath in, but I run on. Through the mangroves, thinking maybe I will get stuck here and drown like the horse in *The Neverending Story*. The mud is thick and it pulls my feet down with every step, but I stumble on. Until I'm at the boat.

I talk to myself so I don't feel like I'm alone. Put my hands on either side of the bow. Push. Slip and hit the side of my cheek, a dull thud in time with my heartbeat. I'm up again and hear a low grunt, frightening until I realise it is *me* moving that boat out and into the rising water.

Maman, je te ramène à la maison!

I hear Mum sing her favourite Françoise Hardy song, 'Le temps de l'amour'. How I've waited to hear her voice! We'll sail across the sea faster than anyone ever thought possible. But then she is gone because the wind has grown spiteful and stolen her voice away. I throw all my weight into my arms and push the boat forward. Leaves and branches whip my face, dirty air slams into my eyes so that I can only squint. The boat feels heavy like a marble statue.

Taken by my struggle, God decides to intervene. I push again, and the boat slides forward, light as a feather. I hop in and the water floats the rowboat into the channel.

Can hardly see for all the needle rain hitting me in the face but I know he's coming. Got a ninth sense about Joni: one-third more than usual.

And when I look back, there he is running through the mangroves with Augie Belle tight under one arm.

The water is watching and it wants to play a game. I hear a whisper travel across its surface until it's close enough to hear: 'You cannot have me if I cannot have the boy.'

Before I can stop him Joni jumps straight into the water and disappears underneath. He's too little to know this night sea has a black heart.

I jump out of the boat and swim under the water all

on one breath, reach out and grab his foot; tangled by the reeds that think it's all a game too.

Quick! His lungs are small and about to burst.

Finally I drag him up to the surface. Then he's like a newborn and I am tortured until a gasping splutter brings him back into the world.

We collapse on the bank letting our desperate lungs fill up with air. In this moment there's only me and him, arms and legs wrapped around trying to crawl inside one another. The storm is so ferocious all the trees want to escape too, falling over this way and that, branches cracking loudly. They fall so close I feel a twig catch the side of my face so I pick Joni up and we scramble through the falling forest.

The path has gone and I can't tell if I'm heading in the right direction. I think I see the house, a large shadow in the distance and figures calling our names. So I do not see what is coming and maybe the tree is already asleep before it hits the ground but it takes me with it.

Back of the head, crack like a cricket ball hit for six.

I fall onto my knees so I don't squish Joni. There's no pain so I must be all right even though there's a golf-ball lump on the back of my head. I touch it and then look at my hand. Covered in red. That magic water inside my body is leaking out, and when I see all that blood, I just can't be brave anymore.

I hear that wolf of mine yell at me: 'This is what you get for trying to steal a child away!'

Now the ocean won't set us free. It will keep me here so I can be punished.

Maman, aide-moi!

That is the last thing I say before I die.

29

Chickpea

They say it was a once-in-a-decade storm. William's house was a wreck; seven windows broken and half the roof missing. Ended up in the neighbour's pool two doors down. I don't know where I went for the next three months. The clock kept ticking over but someone had forgotten to wind me up. There's a throat tube to help me breathe and my brain's been switched off so I can heal. Every day another medical forecast. She might wake up, she might keep sleeping. Or you might turn the machine off and let her go forever. Even though I couldn't understand what they said, I knew they were there. In the morning it would be William. He would read to me. I could hear the pages turn and his soft steady voice. In the afternoon Aunty Cecilia and Jules would take turns like they'd popped over for arvo tea to tell me how the tomatoes were doing this year. Sometimes they would cry. Then they would keep talking because that's what the doctors had told them to do. To let me know I wasn't alone. And one time Pat was there too. Didn't say much but he stayed for the longest time. Then the room got cold and I went down deeper into myself.

After a while even though my eyes were shut I could see shapes: blobs of light and shadows when the sun flickered across the window. One day I feel William hold my hand and stroke my fingers. I could *feel* again. Like hands are a new invention and the doctors have just strapped one on. People don't sound like they're talking underwater anymore. I can hear William's words the clearest, he tells me stories. They're mostly the ones he tells Joni, but I don't mind. One is about a spider-man. Not the red and black one who's really Peter Parker. This one's called Anansi. Some people call him Mr Nancy and that makes me laugh even though my mouth can't move. Mr Nancy makes the rain come and decides how wide the rivers can flood. He makes it all possible: the sun, moon, stars, day and night. I squeeze William's hand. Then hear his chair scrape as he runs out of the room. People come in and speak my name. People I don't know and do not want to see so I stay inside myself. I don't know if it's two minutes, hours, or days later, but the next time William takes my hand I open my eyes because his is the face I want to see for the first time again. So I'd know I hadn't died after all.

He just stares at me with wonder and wobbly eyes.

'Chickpea.' The inside of my mouth is dry and the word feels wooden.

William's shadow falls over my face as he leans forward, eyes wide open. 'I couldn't hear you, bubby,' he whispers so my ears don't crack.

'Channa...means chickpea,' I say.

And then his eyes go all crinkly like they're gonna fall in on themselves.

'You're my channa.' Massaging my hand again, he's smoothing out the fleshy spot right at the base of the thumb.

I have no idea why I kickstarted my mouth up again with a chickpea. I don't even like hummus. I close my eyes, and do you know what I think about? Snowflakes, slowly falling onto my tongue.

When I find out Christmas has come and gone I am devastated. I imagine the table covered in crackers and the box of Darrell Lea assorted chocolates and candies, then the turkey and ham and peas and curried-egg sandwiches that Mum would make just for me. Even though I have no clue what William's spread was like, I've missed out. Hadn't even thought about what present I'd wanted and wishing is the best part of all.

William brings in a little mini plum pudding that he'd made just for me and Nurse Wendy gives us some custard to have with it. My tummy remembers all the food it has missed and I eat William's half too. Then he gives me a once-in-a-lifetime present—a sterling silver fork that was 103 years old from Germany. It used to belong to Father Ewald and it was very strong because it had withstood two wars and a wall falling down. And there is also a gift from Aunty Cecilia and Jules: Tina Arena's latest and greatest hits. Finger on the pulse, thanks very much ladies. Nurse Olivia even brings in a tape player so I can listen to it.

While I was asleep I figured out that Paris and my dad had always been a dream, real and imagined. But I am awake now. That night my metal fish had been in my pocket. Had I wanted to take it with me across the seas? I can't say. But it pressed through my pocket and imprinted scales on my skin like I was a living fossil. Those small half-moons, a perfect kind of miracle. I lost it in the water, either trying to get the boat into the ocean, or Joni out of it. It's swimming in that wide-open sea now, whether it wants to or not. I hope it means that Dad is free too. Despite what he's done I miss him all the same because he will always be part of me. But, on the other side of the storm, I feel like we have let each other go.

The boy next to me here on the ward—Marvin—got burnt when a pot of boiling water fell on his arm when he was four. And he still needs operations when his skin gets too tight. His dad is a bikie who sometimes visits with his leather-jacket mates. They all have moustaches and wear sunnies even when they are inside. Marvin's dad says he'll take me for a ride on his bike when I am better.

I have to have rehab to rejig my muscles and bones on account of them hibernating for so long. I have a massive splinter deep down in my finger, a piece of that boat that might never come out. Everything hurts and sometimes even though I know what I want to say, I borrow the wrong words and they don't make any sense.

They stitched my head up pretty good, but they still can't tell me how much blood I've lost. I ask them to check my magic water levels, but the doctor says they don't have a machine for that. Which is not true. When you spin a test tube of blood round and round, the magic water part always floats to the top. Then come the white blood cells, and then the red. I figure I was asleep all that time so my body could make more of everything.

Joni comes now that I am awake and we go to the kids' room and play Connect 4 or Monopoly. I let him pass

GO whenever he wants. We never talk about that night. But I won't ever forget the look on Joni's face watching me try to leave. The water had no intention of taking me out to sea. And it lured Joni to remind me of who I could not live without. Now I'm not sure if it was being cruel to be kind. But I do know the more time I spend with Joni the better my wounds are healing.

William plays games with me too, brings in his old domino set most days he visits.

'Anyone for a half D?' He smiles and nods like I'm in on some joke of his from 1963. That's what they used to say in Kitty Village, his hometown back in Guyana. Looking for someone to play six rounds of dominoes which is kind of like a set of tennis. Game-set-match without the 40–loves and sweat. William moves his dominoes round like he's gonna do some magic cup trick instead. Shields them with his hand so I can't peek. I don't really care if he sees my dots so I lay them flat on the table instead. You're supposed to have three people playing, but we still make it work.

Some days a headache thumps behind my eyes so loud I have to have everything dark and lie with a wet cloth on my forehead.

William talks to me about time. How we set our watches, hearts, brains and feet by something that is just an idea. Only real because we make it so. I am only here because of yesterday clouds ripping apart the sky, throwing me into a broken-hearted today that might never ever change. Maybe time will run out and the future will never turn up. There is only one thing I know for sure. William has been my timekeeper all along. Waiting and hoping that I would someday find my way to him.

One day when the arvo tea trolley has been round I tell William I am sorry for it all. He puts down his Kingston biscuit and thinks for a long time, rubbing my hand back and forth.

'Life is about making and losing connections. But too many people go.'

William went to church a lot while I was in hospital, prayed to God and Buddha and Ganesh the elephant for good measure. Then he'd go for a drive until he got to the Wylark River, park the car and walk alongside. Follow its path round corners and bends 'til he didn't know which way was forward and which way was back.

Black skin and water. I'd got them both wrong, thinking they'd betrayed me. Neither of them is good or bad, but fear likes to make things simple.

William says I can't keep secrets like the boat anymore and that I can talk to him about whatever I am feeling. Sometimes he might just listen. He knows about that pain in my gut thinking I'd let Mum down, so I promise to try. When we watch a one-day cricket match in the kids' room, I practise not keeping a secret. I tell William that sometimes I wish a duck upon Brian

Lara before he even makes it to the crease, 'cause the Aussies will always be my dream team even though the Windies rule the world. He smiles and says we'll have to work on that.

Being asleep for so long changed a lot of things. I am more familiar to myself. It feels like waiting in line for ages only to find that all the tickets have been sold. You see another movie anyway and it's actually okay. There are strange bits that don't make sense but you watch it 'til the end 'cause the last song is quite catchy and it makes you feel good.

When I go home I am still in recuperation, which means that I can sit on the couch and eat ice cream and get Joni to put my apple cores in the bin so that I don't have to get up. Joni snuggles in with me and watches cartoons and even lets me braid his hair because it's getting really long. Any time someone comes near him with a pair of scissors he runs into my wardrobe. I don't mind if he goes in there. He brings me the rest of his buttons and I sew them all over the holes in Augie Belle's fur so the stuffing won't come out. As well as being practical it also makes Augie Belle ten years younger. He looks pretty and interesting for the first time in his life. And when I sew each button on I tell Joni another secret about water. Whenever he feels sad and misunderstood like you can when you don't use your words, he points to a button on Augie Belle and I tell him the secret again. Sit there for ages, he would, listening to all those water facts and stats:

Blue pearl: hot water freezes faster than cold water.

White swirl: water is the only liquid with a memory.

Black jet black: people can drink up to forty-eight cups of water a day. Forty-nine and you might internally explode.

Purple and pink dots: water boils faster in Colorado than in New York.

Big fat orange: four million people die every year from toxic water.

Soon enough those buttons make Joni go to sleep (except for big fat orange which he didn't point to much) and I put my hand on his chest, let it rise up and down.

One day I tell William I want to go back into the mangroves where it had all gone so wrong. Maybe Mum had made it without me, I say. But when we walk down the path there are pieces of the boat everywhere, smashed, splintered, shattered.

'I think...she's wherever you choose her to be.' William clasps his hands together and looks to the ground.

There is room for the sadness we feel. Might get smaller and lighter but it will always be there like a stain you wash and wash but can't get out.

I don't go to the mangroves after that. I follow William's river instead. Down near the old convent where girls my age used to wash sheets all day because nuns said they'd done shameful things and had to clean out their soul. Down to the river that soaked up their sorrow and William's all the same, 'cause it had seen him pray through my sickness. He said with all his tears it doubled in size. Just between you and me, I think William's poetic licence is out of date. Rivers can only rise with water from the sky. And Mr Nancy the spider-man is in charge of that.

We still walk that river but not with words or wishes. We watch the birds call for one another. The snap of branches as they jump through bushes collecting sticks for their nests. The sound of someone close, unseen in the trees. We watch the sun retire for the night sending shadows soft and long across distant fields. I know in those moments we are both scared of things to come. But as that wolf of mine would say, there's no point running from yourself 'cause wherever you go, there you are.

When he hears I am out of hospital Pat comes. He's got himself a new job recycling cardboard boxes. Things can change just like that and become better than they were before.

I don't know why but I stay in my room when William tells me he's arrived. Even though I've changed my outfit and done my hair in a ponytail I need to change again. Green corduroy skirt and striped pink T-shirt. The ridges in the skirt go up and down and the T-shirt stripes across. My head is all cloudy and I feel colourblind. I creep out and stand in the hallway, watch as William shakes Pat's hand and his head bobs a bit with all the mateness going on between them.

'Cuppa tea?'

'I'd murder a coldie.'

'Right you are, long trip.'

And they both drink their beer straight from the bottle.

They look like one of those TV cop duos: one short and skinny and the other with a potbelly and bony fingers.

'Aha!'

My stripey/ridgey camouflage fails and William spots me. I inch forward. The wall is cold on my back 'cause William's had the air-con blasting all day. He'd rather be cool and broke than hot and rich.

'G'day stranger.' Pat stands up and holds out his hand. William says he has some more filing to do which is not true.

I run back into my bedroom. Joni's disease must be contagious because I cannot speak.

After a while Pat knocks but doesn't wait for an answer. Comes straight in. Rude.

'How's the head? William says you're doing really well.'

'Maybe I am, what's it to you?' I don't know why I'm being so standoffish but everything feels starchy between us. Pat sits on the bed and talks about how he's cleaned up his act, that he's working for the Salvos with the boxes and they've got him in a program where people talk every week about their gambling. Got his fridge back too. He pauses to rub his neck, then says he's moved into a nice two-bedroom flat and made up the spare just for me for when I visit. Put a Johnny Farnham poster on the wall. I didn't tell Pat I already knew. That I visited him when I was asleep for all those months. Saw all the cleaning up and clearing out. Lying awake at night in cold sweats. Taking flowers to Mum's grave. Even going to the library and listening to French language tapes. *Bonjour, ça va toi? Ça va bien, toi?* The burning shame as he hands his photo to the lady at the RSL club, anywhere that's got a pokie machine: 'I'm a recovering addict. Please do not let me enter.' Taking the double shift every weekend just to keep temptation at bay. That he wanted only to love and be loved the right and honest way. And the only right thing to do was to look after me.

'I talked to Mrs Whatsher…your teacher back home and she said there's still a place for you there. Things could be like normal again.'

246

It sounds great because I miss my old friends, even Amanda Pearson who was never nice to me and talked through her nose like she was always whining. But when you get older you have to make tough life choices. Like how and where you choose to live it. So I put my quiet voice on and tell Pat I'd wanted the same thing too, but it couldn't ever be that way. Pat had brought me to William who'd brought me to the hoatzin bird who'd brought me to Joni, and that's where the journey ends. Can't reverse time because everything that's happened has changed who you are and what you know.

Pat's shoulders slump and for a moment that movie *The Wizard of Oz* flicks into my head. Why the hell did that tin man want a heart? Didn't he know that people can punch the love out of you, even if they don't use their hands?

'Oh. Righto. Yeah. You see, the thing is…'

What Pat wants to say is he didn't know he needed me until I was gone. I know because that is the same way I feel about him. But you can't be in two places at the same time.

'Pat, I have to tell you something.' I know it will come as a surprise but William said I couldn't keep those big secrets anymore. 'I'm a full half-black now. And it's okay 'cause William's put me back in the real world.'

I tell Pat I want to stay where I am so I can make tinned spaghetti jaffles with William and brush his hair with a special frizz comb because he says it feels like heaven. To dance up front when Jules plays at the pub first Sunday of the month. Draw animals on Joni's back when he can't get to sleep. I also have to stay in case somewhere along his own timeline Joni feels skin shame and looking at his reflection feels like stepping on shattered glass. I'll try and suck his shame out like venom from a snakebite. I need to be here so I can remind him that we are fine, even if it doesn't always feel that way.

When the Olympic Games are on, Joni and I sit on the couch and drink hot chocolate. William shows us when the athletes from Guyana came out. I cheer and whoop even though there are only five of them and they have never won anything except way back in 1980 when we got a bronze medal for boxing at the Moscow Olympics. I'm a lover not a fighter so am a bit disappointed to hear that. But you won't believe this: that boxer's name was Michael Anthony *Parris*—what are the chances?

I take Pat outside and down to the back gate. William and I had made a cross out of the boat wood, stuck it in the ground and put ferns all around the bottom because Mum always thought they looked exotic. I made a picture of us in the boat sailing across the sea and covered it in contact so it was waterproof. Then we stapled it to the cross.

Pat stares at the cross for a long time. I say he hasn't lost me, that I will always be just down the phone. Pat says half the time it wasn't him talking; it was his addiction that made him cranky and short-tempered, unable to listen and ask what I needed. But that he is practising to be better. I show him that splinter of wood from the boat, still stuck way down in my finger.

'It'll come to the surface in its own time,' he says. Pat holds my hand and kisses that splintered finger. Nothing is forever and I can always change my mind if I feel like it, that's what he says, still not believing he's come all this way only to go home without me.

I didn't tell him that some things *are* forever. Like statues made out of marble.

We go back inside and while Pat finishes his beer I have a can of Solo. I chink my can on his bottle and we say cheers at the very same time. Aunty Cecilia and Jules and Joni come because they want to say hi. Their hellos don't really have a goodbye so Pat is stuck there until after dinner, which he says is okay because the food on the plane is rubbish and it's the last flight out. Everyone is talking and Joni is on my lap twiddling Augie Belle's ear over his own. I see that Mum was right. My skin brings together different people and places. Pat and I nod at each other.

'How you goin'?'

'I'm goin' all right.'

Later I sit with Pat out on the front steps while he waits for his taxi. The moon has come out to say goodbye, big and round like a spotlight shining down on the front porch and leaving the rest of the street a patchwork of shadows. I know Pat's trying to keep those floodgates closed.

'When you're lonely, find the moon, Pat. I'll be watching it too.'

I wait as the taxi heads off down the road, hear it on the gravel for a good while after. And I let the cicada drone turn my sadness into static.

Back inside I sit on the couch where Pat had been. It's still warm.

William's eaten too much again and he rubs his stomach. 'I need a magic cure for this damned heartburn.'

'It's called restraint,' says Aunty Cecilia. 'As in slow down with those Turkish Delights I know you stash in your sock drawer so I won't find them. Seriously, who does your laundry, Dad?!'

I say maybe we have some restraint in the bath-room cabinet. Everyone laughs which is inappropriate because you have to take your health seriously.

Then Joni says he knows where it is. Out of the blue Joni cashes in on those words he's been storing up. I knew he'd been listening all along. He got a glass of water, put it down next to William and whispered in his ear.

'The magic,' William says as he looks up at Aunty Cecilia and Jules who can't believe what they're hearing.

'He says the magic is inside the water.'

There are tears in everyone's eyes, but I just roll mine 'cause I've been saying that for years.

Epilogue

Sometimes I can still hear that wolf inside of me, howling quietly. Like he's getting smaller and wants someone to hear him before he disappears altogether. That wolf is sad because his words are fading into the past. We're always losing time and love, I tell that wolf. But he doesn't reply.

I don't really know if Mama ever got back home. She is with me but she has also disappeared. Now I think of being inside that painting she used to stare at in the art gallery, where the sheep is crying over her dead baby in the snow. I get goosebumps because the wind is howling all around. I'm crouching right next to the sheep feeling like that lamb of hers is mine too, and the world is empty apart from our grief. It doesn't matter that I'm human and she's a sheep; we have lost the same part of ourselves. Maybe with time I'll be somewhere else in that picture, further back and out of sight. Down the hill where a warm fire burns on. I'll sit by the window knowing I am safe because any sound in the night is too far away to hear.

It's Tuesday and I'm expecting a call from Pat. I have a feeling he's gonna let me know about the special someone his heart has found. I will let him tell me even though that blue-faced, orange-mohawked hoatzin bird still flies over his place keeping watch for me. No one knows the shape of their heart until someone else steps inside; let them see how deep and wide it really is.

I can hear the phone ringing now. That Pat O'Brien, he's right on time.

Thanks to Mum, Dad, Andreas, Edwin, Kez, Nina, Jess, Monica, Dr Jeanine Leane, Aunty Maureen and Lucy the magpie.